I0566040

When
the
Bedposts
Shake

GARY LEE VINCENT

Burning Bulb
PUBLISHING

When The Bedposts Shake: Ring of the Succubus
By **Gary Lee Vincent**

Burning Bulb Publishing
P.O. Box 4721
Bridgeport, WV 26330-4721
United States of America
www.BurningBulbPublishing.com

Cover designed with licensed elements from Shutterstock, Inc.
 - ID 243366034 by Kuznechik and ID 150993854 by Irina_QQQ.

First Edition.

Paperback Edition ISBN: 978-1-948278-15-7

Printed in the United States of America

Also by Gary Lee Vincent

Novels
PASSAGEWAY
BELLY TIMBER
ATTACK OF THE MELONHEADS

Darkened—The West Virginia Vampire Series
DARKENED HILLS
DARKENED HOLLOWS
DARKENED WATERS
DARKENED SOULS
DARKENED MINDS
DARKENED DESTINIES

Nonfiction
THE WINNER, THE LOSER
AGELATIONS
CONFIGURATION MANAGEMENT

Musical Releases
100 PERCENT
PASSION, PLEASURE, & PAIN
SOMEWHERE DOWN THE ROAD

PART 1
JACK

CHAPTER 1

Jack

"It's a great place," Mr. Bannering told Jack Crannson, while handing him the additional keys to the house he'd recently purchased. "It's well situated and everything—and you're certain to love the lake itself." Then he'd paused as if wondering whether to go on. "Just ensure you leave that north bedroom door locked."

Mr. Bannering was the house's previous owner. He looked almost as old as the building he'd sold Jack. Both seemed to have come into existence sometime in the 1950s.

He and Jack were sitting in Jack's office, up on the third floor of Atwood Engineering, a modern building in the prestigious White Oaks industrial plaza in Bridgeport, West Virginia. Mr. Bannering was on his way south to live in Florida with his daughter and her husband. He'd moved out of the old house two months ago and since then had been living with a cousin of his. Jack had moved into the house two weeks ago.

"But why?" Jack asked. Now that he thought back, he recalled that when the realtor had driven him out to look the building over, they'd not been able to get into that northern upstairs room; nor into the loft either. The loft latch had rusted shut, but Mr. Bannering had claimed to have lost the keys to the north bedroom. Since moving in, Jack had planned on getting a carpenter to force the door and change the lock, but with three other bedrooms to choose from, he'd not been in any hurry.

"It's complicated to explain," Mr. Bannering said.

"At least try," Jack said. "You must agree it's really strange to sell someone a house and place restrictions on its use after they've bought it." Then, seeing Mr. Bannering's face take on a look of resignation (as if he'd known better than to start this thread of conversation in the first place), he tried to humor the old fellow. "I'm curious, that's all."

He grinned. "At least let me know if you've something hid away in there that's going to kill me."

Mr. Bannering smiled thinly. "It's just an old tale; one dating from the seventies. Something about that north bedroom."

"What's in there?"

"Nothing. Just an old bed." Then Mr. Bannering laughed. "Look, forgive my rambling, son. Maybe I'm just an old fool now, but . . . I've kept that door locked for forty years now and never had cause to regret it. I never went in there myself nor did I let anyone who entered the house go in that room either. The other three bedrooms were enough for Mildred—that's my late wife—and me and our daughter Tracy to live in. In a way, after a while I came to view myself as a sort of keeper of what that bedroom housed." The old man paused and nodded to himself, his old face as creased as his memories. "Yeah, I felt that I was keepin' everyone in town safe."

"So what was in the room? I mean rather, what *is* in there that you're so concerned about?"

"Well . . . see . . ."

But their conversation was over. They'd run out of time. Jack had a business appointment waiting—the client had already arrived. Mr. Bannering had to hurry away too. He was on his way to the Harrison Marian Airport; his Uber cab was waiting downstairs. He'd merely stopped by as a favor. Last night, while sorting out which of his property to take with him on his journey and what to ditch or leave in storage, he'd found a ring of spare house keys that he'd forgotten to hand over to the house's new owner. So he'd called Jack and arranged to drop the keys off at his office on his way out of town.

Jack saw the old man to the office door. "Well, thanks for stopping by, sir. And I'm really grateful for to you for bringing the keys here for me. But I really don't see how I won't use that north bedroom. I don't mean right now," he added quickly. "But with time, because of its location, I'm thinking I might make it my study. All my work stuff is currently downstairs and I'd prefer an upstairs room with a view of the sky."

Mr. Bannering tried once more before leaving: "Well, I can't tell you what to do with your own property, son. But . . . if you do use the room, at least *try* not to sleep in the bed?"

And then the old man was gone; off south to Florida where the sun would warm his old bones.

Mr. Bannering shuffled off towards the elevator. Jack waved in the woman who wanted to see him. The lady represented one of the other contractors for the Melas project, a town recently devastated by a flood.

While she seated herself in the chair opposite his desk, Jack pondered the old man's words. Maybe Mr. Bannering was going senile. Yes, that would be a valid reason for him spouting such nonsense. God knew the old guy had to be at least 80 years old now. Well, he looked that old anyway. Good thing he was off to Florida then.

"Not use a room in a house I just bought?" Jack muttered to himself. "That's a completely weird instruction. And one impossible to adhere to."

"Huh?" the blonde woman opposite him said. "What did you say?"

"Sorry," Jack apologized, realizing he'd been thinking aloud. "Nothing serious. Just some nonsense old-timer superstition."

He smiled at his client and concentrated on his work.

***

Jack Crannson was in his early thirties. He was of average height and weight, had ash blonde hair, green eyes, and a generally happy disposition. A calm and cautious man.

Jack was an architect. He 'owned' Atwood Engineering (as in, he was both the senior partner and owned the lion's majority of company shares). Atwood Engineering was currently involved in the reconstruction of the town of Melas, a place situated 30 miles east of Bridgeport along Route 50. The Melas project was an ongoing one, though the reconstruction's sponsor, a billionairess by the name of Jackie Nixon, had recently vanished without a trace.

***

Jack Crannson was by no means a superstitious man. Which was why one of the first things he did after getting home that evening was check if any of the keys Mr. Bannering had brought over fit the lock on the north bedroom door.

One of them did. Jack opened the door, turned on the lights and had a look at the place. The old man had been right. There was nothing of note in the north bedroom. All it contained was an old bed, an antique lady's dresser, and the drapes over the windows.

Jack stood there, thinking. Now he felt better. Now he felt like he owned this house. Even though he couldn't access the loft yet, that was a different case altogether: it wasn't because he'd been scared off entering there. Not because he feared the bogeyman getting him if he disobeyed Bannering's warning.

He grinned. *How can a guy feel like he owns a place, if he lets the previous owner's mania restrict his movements?*

He saw nothing of interest in the bedroom. It was just an ordinary room. Dusty floor and furniture; lots of cobwebs in the corners. Nothing extraordinary to worry himself or Bannering over. This place just needed some cleaning, fresh air and fresh wallpaper.

After deciding he'd handle the cleaning later, Jack left the room. He left the door unlocked. Maybe he'd throw out the old bed. No, he'd keep it. Samantha liked old stuff like that.

Jack had a lot on his mind. He quickly forgot his conversation with the old man. Which, in retrospect, was a really unwise thing to do.

CHAPTER 2

Jack's Romantic Crisis

Jack Crannson always had a lot on his mind. And most of what he had on his mind was work. He worked really hard at making Atwood Engineering successful. Actually, he'd already made Atwood Engineering successful. Now he just worked to keep it successful.

No. To be honest, Jack Crannson just worked because he was addicted to work.

"You work too hard," his doctor said. Jack disagreed.

His wife Samantha also said he worked too hard. Jack always smirked at her comments. A textbook illustration of the pot calling the kettle black. If anything, Samantha worked harder than he did. At least he liked to think she did.

Staring at the window from his second-floor bedroom, which overlooked his new front yard, Jack sighed. And all that damn work, where had it led them both to? Separate beds and lives; separate paths and now separate homes.

What's the point of work if your careers pull you into two irreconcilable directions? So yes, we've both got fat bank accounts, and we're both very successful and all. Maybe if we'd had kids they'd have been sufficient glue to bind us together? He sighed again. *But I was never around and besides, Sam doesn't want any rug rats. If she'd wanted some, if . . . if . . . if . . .*

He'd told Samantha he'd bought this old house on a whim, a hideaway for them both whenever the stress of work grew too great. But she wasn't fooled in the least. Samantha was smart. She knew the real reason he'd bought this old place in Bridgeport's Maple Lake area, was so they wouldn't have to live together anymore.

Yes, the lake was gorgeous to look at and had fish, and would be fantastic to swim in during these warm summer months, and those neighbors she'd met on her visits there all seemed friendly sorts, but . . .

7

But surely no one who merely wanted a 'hideaway' bought a place in town, right next to their place of work. Nor did they (if all they aimed for were relaxing weekends with their spouse) purchase somewhere which ensured they'd see her as little as possible, like this one did. (The couple's jointly-owned home was fifty miles away from Bridgeport, up north in Cheat Lake.)

They'd discussed a separation more than once. Neither of them wanted one though.

How the hell can a marriage disintegrate when you love the other person? You're both in love and your marriage is falling apart? You love one another and yet can't stand each other?

It was a huge puzzle. A question with seemingly no answer. Jack Crannson wondered which had gotten more upsetting: the silences because they had nothing to say to each other; or the arguments that had resulted from their not saying anything to one another when they should have. Or was it the loneliness? Yes, above all he'd begun feeling isolated. For ages now, while lying beside Samantha at night, he'd felt like he was the only one in the bed.

CHAPTER 3

Jack

It was Saturday morning. Jack didn't have anything planned for today. No friends, no visits.

And meanwhile Samantha, a private investigator, was up in Connecticut working, looking for some teenage girl who may or may not have run away from home. Actually, this was a relief to Jack. It meant there was no chance of her stopping by to make him feel guilty for deserting her.

After a while Jack smiled to himself. All the signs pointed to this being one of those rare weekends when he could relax. He decided to walk through the neighborhood and find somewhere where he could have a quiet coffee.

***

Jack put off his walk when it began raining. He stood by his open bedroom window and watched the water come down, not leaving his post even when gusts of wind blew raindrops in his face. What mostly held his attention was the lake opposite. He enjoyed the dancing patterns the sheets of falling water produced on the water's surface.

Finally though, the rainfall got too heavy to endure. And besides, the bedroom carpet was getting soaked.

After shutting the window, Jack left the bedroom. He'd decided to go watch TV downstairs—the living room set was much larger than the bedroom one—sports looked much better on it.

Stepping from his bedroom (the south one) into the hallway brought him face to face with the north bedroom door. The door was ajar. He stood shocked for a moment, wondering who'd opened the door, then remembered he'd been the one, last night. Then another even more bothersome thought came to his mind:

Just assuming for a minute that Mr. Bannering was telling the truth—just assuming he was—why on earth would he leave an empty room locked for forty years? . . . And . . . and one that he and his wife would be seeing every single time they stepped out of their own bedroom at that.

Try as he might, Jack couldn't answer that question. Abandoning say, the downstairs guest room made some sense—one needn't proceed that way every day—but a room you saw each morning and night?

No . . . there's more to this than meets the eye.

Jack found that he was shivering. *Shit—now I've gone and spooked myself!*

The rain was coming down loud and noisily now, pounding on the roof. This may have contributed to Jack Crannson's sudden unease. Because now, for the first time since buying this building, he felt worried. Suddenly, Jack felt as if that room at the end of the hallway with the slightly-ajar door contained horrible things.

Stop it—there's nothing there!

Despite which thoughts, he hurried along the hallway and shut, then locked the door to the north bedroom.

Then he backtracked and hurried downstairs to pour himself a drink of brandy.

It wasn't until he'd found a Celtics versus Cavaliers 2018 NBA playoffs rerun that the tension left him. And by then Jack was on his third brandy. He tended not to drink this early in the day, but . . . today seemed to demand drinking.

In the break between the third and fourth quarters of the basketball game, Jack pleasantly considered what he'd bought:

The Bannering house was large and roomy, possessing two floors and a loft.

Downstairs there was a large living room, a dining room and kitchen. Jack had also converted a back room into both his home office and a guest bedroom.

Upstairs were three other bedrooms with attached bathrooms and a small study. All-in-all it was a nice house. It had also been a bargain. As far as Jack could tell, Mr. Bannering's daughter and son-in-law hadn't wanted it for some reason. And the old man was apparently too close to the grave to care about turning a profit on the sale.

Outside, the building was painted a stark bone-white, with black roof shingles. Its large windows reflected the sun. The attached garage had space for two cars; at the moment one of those parking spaces was taken up by Jack's silver Kia Sorento SUV. Both the front and rear yard were large, and there were just sufficient trees around the property to give it a feeling of solitude that wasn't isolation.

Maple Lake, the body of water from which this area of town got its name, lay right at the foot of Jack's driveway, on the other side of Maple Lake Road.

CHAPTER 4

Jack

After the Cavaliers won the playoffs game by 87 points to 79, Jack muted the television. It was still raining; looked like it would keep up all morning. Jack sat watching an ID Discovery program for a while, then decided to get up and pour himself another drink.

It was after doing so, in a lull in the rain noise, that he became aware of another sound coming from upstairs.

At the time Jack heard this other noise, he was halfway back to his chair, this time with the brandy bottle in hand.

He froze and listened. The sounds (as there were a sequence of them) continued. The best Jack could liken it to was the sort of noises an unlatched porch screen door would make while being knocked about by the wind. *Bang, bang bang!* Not overly loud, but just loud enough to be irritating . . . and borderline scary.

Jack stopped and considered. The porch analogy made sense if the noise was coming from *outside*. But from overhead? And inside the house for that matter?

He poured himself some more brandy, drank half of it, then climbed the stairs to go investigate the rather spooky sound.

Once upstairs he immediately saw the cause of the noise. The door to the north bedroom was open again. It was swinging to and fro just like in Jack's previous 'screen door' analogy. Each time it hit the door jamb, it somehow didn't quite lock but instead sprang right back to swing shut again.

Jack stood there staring at it. He remembered locking that door. He'd also left the key (and key ring) in the lock. So, why was the door now open, and not just open, but with its key lying on the floor?

And the bedroom door kept swinging back and forth as if one of the bedroom windows was open and letting in the rain and wind.

Jack started to go investigate, then decided to go get his gun first. It just might be that someone had broken into his house. Maybe even one of those kids who lived next door, though why anyone would try to rob someone during a rainstorm was beyond him.

But still, better safe than sorry.

With the door clattering behind him, he hurried down the hallway and into his bedroom, and got the weapon out from his nightstand.

It was a Ruger LCP. Samantha, always the cautious and security conscious one, had insisted that he buy it, and also that he learn how to use it. Jack was a peaceful sort of fellow, but he couldn't argue with her logic. The world was full of crazy people, Samantha said, and if you weren't prepared to defend yourself against them, you'd only have yourself to blame when they came knocking at your door uninvited.

So he'd bought the gun and spent time at a shooting range.

Now, Ruger in hand, he made his cautious way back to the north bedroom.

"Hey, who's in there?" he asked from outside the door.

There was no reply.

"Who's inside the room?" Jack repeated nervously. The door was still swinging back and forth, and with the bedroom lights off he couldn't make out a thing in the interior gloom. "Hey, come on out of there or I'm gonna call the cops!"

Once again there was no reply, just the creaking noise each time the door swung open, the bang of its return, and the sound of the rain hitting the roof.

Jack didn't want to enter the bedroom. He thought of calling the police. In situations like this calling the cops was the sensible thing to do; everyone knew that. But two things prevented this. First was the fact that his phone was downstairs next to his drink. And second was the thought of his resulting embarrassment if the cops came and discovered the bedroom was empty; it would look really bad once they smelt the alcohol on his breath. "Drunken Architect Wastes Precious Police Time!" would make great headlines if the papers caught wind of the incident. The police might even book him for making a crank call.

Jack reached out and touched the swinging door.

On contact, he felt a slight shudder in his hand as if he'd been buzzed by an electrical wire, but the door instantly stopped swinging.

That calmed him somewhat. Gun poised to blow any intruder to hell and beyond, he entered the bedroom. Once he stepped inside, his hand quickly found the light switch and flicked it on.

Then he stood and gaped. The bedroom was empty. The drapes were still drawn and there wasn't the slightest shiver of wind coming from anywhere that could account for the door's back-and-forth motion.

Just like it should be, actually, Jack told himself, walking over to sit on the bed. He looked back over at the door, which hadn't moved an inch since he'd touched it.

Almost as if it had merely been summoning him upstairs.

So what the hell just happened? Am I overworked and seeing things, or what? He scratched his head and wondered if maybe, just impossibly maybe, he'd only imagined that he'd locked the door earlier. *Alright, it's possible that I didn't, but . . . but that doesn't make any sense, and yet—*

He'd just noticed something else. Something that he'd not seen when he'd first entered the bedroom last night, though even with the dusty floor, he had no idea how he could have missed something so prominent and obvious:

There was a curving red line (about four inches thick) drawn on the bedroom floor.

He traced the line around the foot of the bed, at first turning where he sat on it and then leaning over the bed's farther edge to keep track of the crimson course. The curving red line was in fact a circle. Someone had drawn a red circle all around this old wooden bed. But why? And now, he also noted something else for the first time: Unlike in usual situations, where a bed tended to be positioned back against one of a bedroom's walls, this bed—and by extension the red ring encircling it—was set right in the middle of the bedroom. He double-checked on this. Yes, the bed was set dead center in the room.

Jack didn't really ponder on this however. He was unable to. All of a sudden it seemed as if his early drinking was catching up with him.

Damn, why the hell do I suddenly feel so tired?

It was a strange kind of tiredness that Jack felt too. Not 'tired' tired, as in when one felt a natural need to sleep, but an insistent compulsion to lay down his head and rest, no matter what. This tiredness grew on him in stages, becoming more irresistible by the second. He was completely unaware of lying back on the bed, and was surprised to find himself suddenly flat on his back. The bed itself felt extremely comfortable, as welcoming as if it had been built and laid specifically for him. The smelly old pillows felt like Samantha's breasts.

Jack now had a sense of dreaming while still awake. He acknowledged his surroundings—the room's walls and ceiling, both sets of pastel-toned drapes . . . and the door . . .

But actually, he couldn't see the door clearly anymore.

There was now a naked woman standing between the foot of the bed and the doorway. He blinked. His eyes weren't playing tricks on him; there *was* an unclothed woman right at the foot of the bed. For a moment she seemed somewhat insubstantial, as if he were imagining her being there, but after that instant of doubt, he realized that she was real.

Jack stared. Now the naked woman was coming towards him. She stepped around the foot of the bed and then, there she was right beside him.

Physically, this woman was perfect. She was tall and slim, with milk-white skin, very large breasts and wide hips. Her hair was shoulder-length and jet-black. Her face? She was exceptionally beautiful, yes, with high cheekbones and sensual lips. But what caught Jack's attention the most at first were her blue eyes. Her eyes were filled with lust. Sexual desire streamed from them like water gushing from a tap. Jack felt trapped by her eyes, tied up in knots by her unmistakable sexual desire for him.

Before he understood what was going on, he was hard as a bone in his shorts.

"Who are you?" he gasped at the dream woman.

"My name is Cali." Her voice was soft, musical and sweet like the tinkling of low-pitched bells.

"What are you?"

Her lips split into a grin that revealed perfect white teeth. "I'm your perfect woman," she replied his query. "I'm the fulfilment of your utmost desires."

This was apparently true. Though this woman—Cali—looked nothing like Samantha, whom Jack had married because at the time *she'd* been his perfect woman, Jack nonetheless felt an intense desire for Cali. He felt as if he'd sell his soul for her, give his life for her. And yet, at the same time, he was scared of her, scared because he felt there was something wrong about her.

His gaze dropped from her exquisite, if cruel face to her big breasts. Her breasts were the size of melons. Her nipples were proportionately large. They also seemed as stiff as his penis. As his eyes took in her voluptuous shape, his penis throbbed fiercely against his shorts. It seemed to have gotten even harder during their brief conversation. He wasn't wearing underpants and, since he was lying on his back, the legs of the shorts slipped down, revealing his erection. Cali stared down at his cock and laughed. She had a delightful laugh, alluring to listen to. Also, he had the clear sense that she wasn't mocking the size of his manhood; on the contrary, she was visibly delighted by the effect she'd had on him.

Jack tried to reach down and cover himself with his hands. But he couldn't. All of a sudden he just felt so damn weak. He couldn't move a muscle. In fact, at the moment it felt as if all the strength in his body was concentrated in his hard and throbbing manhood.

"What do you want with me?" he managed to ask.

"Everything," she replied, pulling his shorts off. "Your body, your soul, your mind, your hard cock, and above all else, your human seed."

She pulled his slippers off his feet and dropped them out of sight, then undid his shirt and slipped that off him too. She flung both his shorts and his pants across the room. Jack watched them flutter and land on the dresser.

Then Cali climbed up onto the bed. She took his penis in hand and stroked it firmly. "What's your name?"

"Jack! I'm Jack Crannson!" he gasped helplessly. Her fingers felt like subtle electricity rippling along his manhood. So sweet, so impossibly sweet!

"Jack!" she moaned softly, kneeling over him then slipping him into her body. She gasped as her vagina swallowed him. "What a delightful name. Oh, Jack. I need you so much!"

Jack didn't reply. He couldn't reply. He felt like he'd died and gone to Heaven. Her vagina . . . never before had he felt like this in his life. Cali leaned forward on him, rubbing her big breasts against his chest as she ground her buttocks on him.

Jack still felt paralyzed. He stared up at her in wonder, gasping in delight as her body triggered ecstasy after ecstasy in his.

"Oh, Jack!" Cali gasped. "I'm coming, Jack!" Her face twisted up with pleasure. She lifted her chest off his, gripped his shoulders with both hands, and then slammed her buttocks down onto his crotch hard and fast, then froze and rode out her orgasm to its end.

She looked gorgeous as she came. Like a sex goddess.

Cali's orgasm ended. "Now, I want you to come inside me, Jack! Fill me with your seed."

By this point, Jack was desperate to ejaculate. His scrotum felt like it was swollen to the size of Cali's breasts, full of semen ready to squirt up into her. Frozen in place as he was and as such unable to assist his sexual release in any way, Jack felt as though he'd die if Cali didn't help him make it right now.

But she'd meant was she said. She had no intent of leaving him handing.

"I want your sperm, Jack!" she repeated, coldly now, as if they were transacting business, not having sex. "Give me your thick dripping male essence."

Then she smiled and resumed moving on him. He gasped with gratitude as her vagina slid up and down on him again. His eyes tracked her lovely breasts and gorgeous face. Her ass rose and fell until he exploded in one of the most intense orgasms of his life. It was certainly the longest orgasm he'd ever had. It seemed to last forever.

"Thank you! Thank you!" he gushed as the torrents of sperm gushed out of him.

Cali grinned down at him and once again he detected a deep-rooted cruelty in her gaze. "The thanks are rather mine, Jack," she said softly in an amused voice. "You have no idea how grateful I am to you for coming to me."

"You're welcome," he gasped breathlessly. "I ain't been fucked like this in ages. Hey, can we do this again sometime?"

She laughed her tinkling laugh again. "Even more often than you want, Jack. Come back any time you like. I'll be here waiting."

As result of this orgasm, Jack now felt even more tired than before. Incredibly so. He felt his eyes closing. He'd fall asleep any minute now. But wasn't he already asleep? Could one sleep while asleep?

"You'll be where?" he asked her desperately. "How can I find you? I want to see you again!" He meant this. He wanted to see her again, no matter what.

"Here in your bed, in your dreams, of course," she replied. "Waiting to satisfy you, like you've never been satisfied by any woman before. Oh, come back to me soon—I'll be expecting you, lover."

Jack's eyes shut to echoes of Cali's sweet, but somewhat cruel laughter.

CHAPTER 5

Jack

Jack woke up. It took him a few minutes to realize where he was. Outside, he could still hear the rain falling. Pitter, patter, pitter, patter.

Okay, I'm upstairs in bed in the north bedroom and . . . damn, what kind of a dream was that?

Jack felt incredibly tired. More tired than he ever had before.

He lay on his back in the dusty, musty bed, pondering the erotic dream. He remembered some of it: A circle on the floor, his lying in bed, a woman of intense and impossible beauty—with creamy skin and flowing black hair—sex with that dream woman . . . and finally an orgasm that had seemed to last a thousand years.

And now he was back in the real world again and wished he was still asleep, dreaming of Cali. *Cali? Oh, what a wonderful and strange name for her to have. But it was just a dream. A wet dream. A wonderful . . . wet dream.*

His balls felt drained, completely empty. He also felt a wonderful sense of satisfaction overlying his tiredness. So he'd clearly ejaculated in his dream. Which seeing as he'd not had sex for nearly six months was alright—(at least he wouldn't have to masturbate), but would also prove messy (since he'd need to wash his shorts and clean up the bed.

With that in mind Jack sat up. It was now that he realized how truly weakened he was. The dream had drained his energy. He sat poised on the edge of the bed with his muscles all trembling like he'd just run a marathon.

How on earth could he be this tired? Especially after just waking up.

Then Jack realized two other things. The first of these was that he was completely naked. A glance around the bed revealed his shorts and shirt were draped over the dresser as if cast away in a hurry.

The dream . . . In the dream Cali had undressed him . . . and then she'd flung his clothes away across the room . . . and they'd landed over there on the dresser. Exactly how they looked now.

That was odd enough. But even odder was how he'd just noticed there was no semen spattered around him. He'd ejaculated for sure—in addition to his testicles feeling empty, his penis had that nice-post coital feeling to it—but he'd not come either on himself or on the bed. The bed covers were as dusty and dry as when he'd entered the room. He didn't even appear to have perspired much.

Jack tried reasoning out what had happened. However, he couldn't think of any rational explanation. This didn't make sense. Yes, he'd dreamt; he knew that for certain. There was no one called Cali. *She's merely something cooked up by my frustrated sexual subconscious to help me get off. I must've have thrown the clothes over across the room myself. Okay, that takes care of that detail. But my come? what happened to my semen?*

Then he also noticed the red circle on the floor. It was bright red; much more red and distinct than the first time he'd noticed it. *And how on earth did I miss seeing THIS last night?*

Too many questions without answers. Jack got to his feet and slipped on his slippers. He crossed the bedroom to the dresser and picked up his clothes. Then, not bothering to dress, he shambled over to the door to leave.

At the door, he remembered his gun. Confused as he was, he felt it would be suicidal leaving the Ruger LCP lying around where an intruder could find it. So he returned to the bed to search for it. He found the gun beneath one of the two pillows.

Gun in hand, Jack exited into the hallway. Each step he took seemed to drain him further. It was incredible how weak he felt. To reach his bedroom he needed to support himself on the wall.

He made the trip okay, got safely to bed and lay down. Then, ten minutes later he got up again and made the trip downstairs to the kitchen. It had occurred to him that he needed food in his belly. Maybe that would fix the tiredness.

It was only when Jack got downstairs and looked at the clock on the living room wall, that he discovered he'd been asleep in the north bedroom for six whole hours.

With that additional puzzle to figure out, Jack Crannson made himself a very late lunch and then sat in the living room staring at the TV. He ate his sandwich and drank his coke (to keep awake) and after a while felt marginally stronger. So maybe he'd just been really, really hungry; that was all.

However, Jack found that he couldn't concentrate on the television. His mind kept going back to his dream. To the woman he'd dreamed about. Cali. Then after a while, because the dream had been a sexual one, Jack's thoughts drifted from Cali to his estranged wife Samantha. How long ago had it been since he and Samantha had had sex? Jack thought it was at least six months ago, maybe longer.

Feeling a sudden need to speak to his wife, Jack picked up his phone and called her. As expected, the call went straight to voicemail. Maybe she was busy; maybe she just didn't want to talk to him. Sometimes it was difficult to tell the difference. Was Samantha busy now—had she involved herself in getting so busy over the years precisely because she sought an excuse to not speak to him?

Disgusted, Jack dropped the phone on the floor, his mind dully registering the smothered sound it made on striking the rug. He'd have preferred to fling the cellphone at the TV in anger, but even overlooking the cost of replacing both devices after making such a childish gesture, his fingers were inexplicably trembling; not from frustrated rage, but rather from the return of that weakness he'd felt so strongly on awakening.

It's almost like we were separated while we were living together, he thought, remembering all those times when he'd wanted to touch Samantha at night, but hadn't dared to because she'd been giving off an intense vibe of not wanting to be touched. Yes, he'd been incredibly lonely, and his sole source of comfort was rejecting him. And that had been long before Samantha—exhausted from work as always—had unilaterally taken to sleeping in the guest room.

The upshot of all this was, that in the past year, Jack had had sex maybe three times, if even that many. God knew he'd had sufficient opportunity to cheat on Samantha if he'd wanted too, but he hadn't done so. Being a successful man naturally drew women to him; many of whom had let him know they were very willing to have fun with him.

In this, Jack felt he was the victim of a serious irony. He'd been faithful to his marital vows, only to, at the end of the day, suffer the same fate as if he'd been philandering to his heart's desire.

How the hell could an honest man who loves his wife wind up . . .

The crash of his sex life was truly was a puzzle to him. *One which*, he glumly conceded to himself, *I seem to have resolved by creating a fantasy lover for myself.*

Jack also clearly remembered telling his dream girl Cali, that he intended coming back for seconds.

Hmph, he smirked, taking a bite of his sandwich. *Fat chance of that happening. Whoever ever dreams up the same woman twice?*

CHAPTER 6

Caspar

When Caspar Jenkins rode his motorbike home that Saturday night he wasn't expecting to see anything exceptional. He was tired and hungry and wanted to eat, sleep, and fall into bed, with or without his girl, Laney, in the bed too.

Caspar was 20 years old. He was tall and gangly, with brown hair and gray eyes. He worked as a pizza delivery boy for the Domino's Pizza place on Bridgeport's East Main Street. He lived up in Maple Lake, but it was a short ride home.

It was ten now, the roads all about deserted. Caspar's bike hummed beneath him as he sped along the Northwestern pike, aka US Route 50.

Thank heavens the damn rain's stopped, Caspar thought. It had rained almost the whole day through, turning pizza delivery into more of a chore than it should be.

The roads were still wet and glittered in the headlight's glow. Caspar swung the bike off the Northwestern pike, raced the short connecting distance along Maple Lake Run Road, then swung south onto the east division of Maple Lake Road.

Maple Lake Road completely enclosed Maple Lake. As Laney had once pointed out in jest, viewed on a map, the lake was erection-shaped and the road made a great condom around it.

Caspar was almost home when he saw the apparition.

At first (as one generally did in these sorts of situations) he thought he'd imagined it. He was nearing the old Bannering house, the building right before his place. He'd unconsciously slowed down. Bannering had recently sold the place, and Caspar, Laney and her brother Dray had helped the new owner move in. Actually, they'd seen the moving van arrive and walked over to lend a hand if required. Mr. Crannson, the house's new owner, seemed a nice sort. He was youngish and friendly, nowhere near as cranky as old Mr. Bannering had been. Laney though he was cute—in an executive way.

That had been two weeks ago.

But now . . .

Now, Caspar Jenkins saw a naked woman standing right at the foot of the Bannering drive. He was so surprised that he skidded the motorbike almost to a halt. Then, once sure his eyes weren't deceiving him, he parked the bike beside the curb and stared. Caspar was 20 after all, and liked naked females as much as the next young fellow in line.

The woman at the foot of the driveway just stood there. Caspar realized that she hadn't noticed him. Which was hard to explain because he was parked less than ten feet away from her, with his motorbike headlights reflecting brightly off the wet sidewalk in front of her.

He gaped at her. She was slim and beautiful, with black hair. Her body was fantastic; great butt, huge fantastic breasts. She looked sexy as hell. She seemed older than him, looked to be about thirty years of age. She had a preoccupied look on her face that was part frustration, part something he didn't recognize. For certain though, she was upset.

For a moment, trying to figure out her trouble, Caspar looked out onto the lake, wondering if there was something out there on the water that was attracting the woman's attention. But no, as far as he could see, both the lake shore and surface were empty of persons or boats. And also, he realized now that the woman wasn't showing the slightest interest in the lake. She wasn't looking at it, but beyond it, seemingly beyond even the buildings on the lake's opposite shore.

He returned his attention from the water to the nude woman again. He was confused as to whether to call out to her or not. She might be in distress. Or she might not be. But if she was fine, what was she doing out here naked at 10 p.m.? She was in luck though, this street didn't see much traffic at the best of times; and after 9 p.m. it was mostly deserted. He looked up the drive, at the Bannering house. The downstairs lights were off, the upstairs ones on. An obstruction of trees in the way meant he couldn't make out whether or not there were any cars parked in the garage.

Meanwhile, the naked woman had begun pacing back and forth across the foot of the drive. Another weird fact: she never stepped out onto the curb, just kept on pacing back and forth over the gravel with a pissed-off look on her face. She'd cross the drive one way, step off into the lawn, walk towards the farther rose bushes, then reverse her steps. Each time she walked back towards Caspar, he was certain she'd seen him there sitting on his bike, but no, she apparently wasn't seeing him, because she'd walk into the grass verge on this side too, abruptly spin around and repeat the action.

She was really hot though—those immense tits on her were just ooh-la-la—so Caspar didn't mind watching her. Just that her actions weren't in any way logical.

Caspar pondered: *Maybe she's drunk?*

Yes, that was most likely the case. And, who the hell was she anyway? Mr. Crannson's wife (Caspar remembered that the man had been wearing a wedding ring)? Or his sister? . . . A stoned house guest? . . . or (considering her state of total undress), a drunken call girl? But Mr. Crannson hadn't looked the type to hire hookers.

Caspar sat there on his bike wondering whether to ride off or not. The nude woman was still standing right by the curb. Now she'd begun feeling the air in front of her. At least that's what it looked like. She'd tap the air, then growl silently as if there was a wall there. It was crazy to see, but Caspar honestly didn't mind too much about that. There was something about this lady that was immensely attracting.

But Caspar felt things were dragging on a bit too long. For him, that is.

Any moment now, this impossibly sexy lady might snap out of her crazed reverie and spot him staring at her. Why she hadn't so far was impossible to deduce. But he knew all good things had to end. And once she did spot him . . . if she was drunk or mad like she seemed now, it would be simple enough for her to denounce him as a rapist.

But then Caspar Jenkins forgot all about that. Because suddenly the woman flickered. Just like that, she blinked out of sight and then reappeared again.

Caspar couldn't believe it. His first thought was that he'd blinked and his eyes and mind had momentarily blacked her out. He was sleepy after all.

But then it happened again. Just like a scene from a sci-fi flick. For the briefest of moments the woman's body winked out of sight, then all of a sudden she was back on the gravel again, seemingly as solid as before.

It was crazy to view and scared the hell out of Caspar.

She's . . . she's . . .

He couldn't even think the word 'ghost.' Instead, he looked back up the driveway at the old house. Yes, tonight the white building looked spooky. Now, he also remembered his girlfriend Laney hinting at something weird about the house, but they'd been getting drunk at the time and she'd not elaborated.

He looked back from the house to the flickering and naked woman. It was only now that he realized he had an erection. His penis was stiff and throbbing in his pants and seemed to have a life of its own.

Then the woman vanished. This time she didn't even flicker. She just ceased being in front of him. He blinked thrice. Yes, she was gone.

Caspar sat there on his bike, staring at the spot where she'd been standing. He was really frightened, his heart thudding. *Did I? Er . . . I didn't, did I?*

Then, he glanced nervously out at the lake. *Maybe when I blinked, she just ran out and leapt into the water?* But he knew that wasn't true. The lake water was still, with not a ripple troubling its surface.

If his eyes doubted the truth of his impossible vision, his body didn't. His penis was still painfully hard in his pants. He grabbed his crotch in confusion. His cock felt so stiff, it felt to him that the penis wanted to burst its way out of his pants and also vanish off to wherever that naked beauty had just vanished to.

Caspar waited for his breathing to ease up and his penis to go down. His breathing normalized. His penis didn't. His dick remained hard.

Nonplussed, knowing he was going to have to masturbate if Laney wasn't in the mood to fuck, Caspar started up his motorbike again and rode the twenty yards home.

CHAPTER 7

The House-sitters

The house Caspar lived in wasn't actually Dray and Laney's. It belonged to the sibling's older sister Karen. But Karen, a US Army major was currently serving at the Torii Station military base in Japan, and her husband and kids had moved there to be with her, so her younger brother and sister were looking after her house for her.

Drayfuss 'Dray' Springer was twenty (same age as Caspar), tall, blonde and a bit fat. He and Caspar Jenkins had been best friends from grade school. Dray was smart as hell but didn't yet know what he wanted to do with his life. So, at the moment he too worked as a pizza delivery boy for Domino's. The other thing about Dray was that he loved video games and was painfully shy where girls were concerned.

On the other hand, his sister Elaine 'Laney' Springer was quite extroverted. She was nineteen, slight in stature, and her blonde hair had hint of brown in it. She was attractive enough and loved Caspar a lot, though he liked sex a bit too much for her liking.

Laney was a chemistry student at West Virginia University, but this was summer—and school was out for the moment—so she was at home taking it easy. She spent her time watching TV, trying not to gain weight, and going for rides with Caspar on his bike when he wasn't working.

***

When Caspar got home this Saturday evening, Dray was sitting on the floor in front of the TV with a game controller in his hand and a half eaten pack of Pringles by his side.

He looked up when Caspar walked in. "Dude, you finally made it home. You get the beers?"

"Yeah," Caspar dropped a Bud Light six-pack beside Dray. He checked out the PS2 video game on the TV—Conflict: Vietnam—then asked: "Dude, where's Laney?"

"In her room." Dray paused the game, got out a beer can from the six-pack and cracked it open. "Thanks for remembering these—you don't know how dry a guy's throat gets while saving the USA from the digital enemy." He gobbled down a handful of Pringles then stared at Caspar's face. "Hey, dude, you alright? You don't look too well."

"I'm fine," Caspar lied. "Just need to rest a bit." He forced a smile. Man, get back to killing those damn Vietcong. I need to ask Laney about something."

Dray nodded and restarted the game.

Caspar walked off through the house. He'd been to tell Dray what he'd seen outside the Bannering house, but then he'd realized it would take a whole lot of explaining and his penis couldn't wait. While conversing with Dray, he'd covered his crotch with a hand so the other young man wouldn't guess what was really up with him.

"Hi, baby," Laney said, when he walked into her bedroom. She shook her cellphone at him. "Hey—you won't believe what Amy Landry just posted on her timeline." Then she gasped. "Hey—wait up a minute! Not now, baby!"

But her boyfriend wasn't waiting. In a single fluid movement, Caspar had unzipped his pants and sprung his erection free. Yes, that felt so much better. Not as good as it soon would though.

Laney stared at the stiff penis. Tonight for some reason, she felt threatened by it. It looked larger than usual, swollen full of angry blood. Still, she felt like she had no choice now; Caspar was already pulling his pants off. His shirt quickly followed. She looked at his face and couldn't help laughing. He looked so damn serious.

Laney sighed. She was wearing a tee shirt and panties. The panties quickly came off. She lay back and spread her legs, watching him slip a condom on. She managed to giggle as he entered her, then gasped in some pain. "Slow down, man, you're hurting me!"

"Sorry," Caspar gasped, but he slowed down. "You don't know how much I fucking need you tonight."

That was fine then. Laney appreciated him thinking of her. "You missed me, babe?" she cooed in his ear, stroking his hair as his thrusts into her sex grew more frenetic.

"Yes, oh hell yes, girl. I missed you like you wouldn't believe."

The sex actually hurt a bit because Laney wasn't properly lubricated, but she endured it. At least he was thinking about her and not some other girl. Just before he came he bent his head and sucked on her breasts. That was enough for her. She rose up into the sensation and managed to match his orgasm with one of her own.

Afterwards, as they lay side by side, Laney stroked his cheek and asked: "Cass, what got into you tonight?"

He grinned. "Oh, nothing baby. I just felt an intense need for your sweet puss." He kissed her. "There's just something about this sexy body of yours that I can't get enough of."

Then while she smiled and licked her lips with delight, he added. "Oh, girl, you're not gonna believe what I just saw out there."

"What, baby?" She felt slightly bothered without knowing why.

He was about to talk, then decided to wait. He shook his head. "Hey, not tonight. I'll tell you and Dray about it tomorrow, if I still believe it myself."

No matter how much Laney pushed Caspar after that, he refused to elaborate on what he'd seen. "No, no, no. I need your bro's take on this too. I need both of you guys' brains working on this"

She shrugged. "So fetch him in here now. Just gimme a few minutes to put on some clothes first."

Caspar shook his head. "Nah, we need Dray's input when he's not busy shooting up some digital universe. And . . ." he gestured in the air with a hand for emphasis, "when he ain't too damn drunk to think straight."

"You seriously ain't gonna tell me tonight?"

"Nope."

She rolled on top of him and pouted sweetly. "C'mon, Cass, gimme a hint of what you saw. Just a li'l one. Please?"

"Uh uh. But I'll give you something else if you like."

"Yeah? What's that? Ooh!" Laney moaned with delight as Caspar slid down her body, trailing his tongue down her belly to her crotch, while at the same time kneading her soft yielding flesh. Finally he arrived at her vagina. Gently parting the lips of her wet sex with his fingers, he dived in with his tongue, lapping at the juicy opening, licking along it from anus to clitoris and back again, while she squirmed deliciously and shifted her buttocks till she felt more comfortable.

He concentrated on her clitoris, wetting two fingers and gently slipping them deep into Laney's vagina. She gasped as the probing fingers entered her body, neither as thick nor filling as his turgid cock had been, but capable of much more manipulation. When, in tandem with his licking and sucking on her clitoris, his gently probing fingers found that special spot inside her pussy, she arched her hips off the bed. She began coming, moaning his name softly.

When her orgasm subsided, she gazed into his eyes. "Come inside me, Cass," she softly urged him. "I want you in me again."

He slipped on a fresh condom and entered her. She held him tight, crushing him against her breasts. They moved in tandem, in a short while finding a gentle rhythm that suited both of them. Excited by the devastating sweetness of her body, Caspar just managed to hold himself back till Laney had had another climax. Then his sperm squirted out of him again, while she wrapped him in both arms and legs and wept out his name.

When the feeling subsided in them, they lay back on the bed again, holding hands and giggling.

CHAPTER 8

Jack

On Sunday morning, Jack woke up feeling somewhat better. He was still inexplicably weak, but shrugged it off as exhaustion. It had been a hard week, he had the Melas downtown shopping center design to approve, and the pair of junior architects he'd tasked with elaborating the details of the building's interior had made a complete mess of the perspectives he'd explained to them. He'd had to sit and fix those details himself. Some things really had to be handled personally.

But still, even if he was exhausted from overwork, Jack didn't understand how the tiredness had crept up on him so suddenly. That was the puzzling thing. Or was that how all breakdowns worked? One moment you felt fantastic and the next you were completely out of it, your health shot to pieces.

But at no time during the week did I push myself too hard. I'm certain of it. Once I'd gotten the layout of those rooms straightened out I handed the floor plan back to Janice and Gary to fill the details in. Or did I . . .

He checked his cellphone. He had a text message from Samantha. Sent at 11:32 last night. She'd apologized for not picking up, said she'd been busy then. She promised to call him today, come hell or high water.

Jack smirked at her promise. It wasn't the first promise she'd make and break.

Feeling hungry, he left his bedroom to go make breakfast. He took his cellphone along with him. He intended on speaking to Samantha today. He understood that she might be angry with him, but he needed to talk to her. Hearing her voice would calm the unease he'd felt since yesterday.

He stared down the hallway at the north bedroom door. It was locked again. He'd made sure to lock it last night. He'd also removed

31

its key from the key ring and secured it in the bottom drawer of his nightstand. That way, even if a thunderstorm blew the roof off the house, there was zero chance of the north bedroom door popping open like it had yesterday.

He made his way to the stairs, took two steps down, then decided to make certain that that north bedroom door was locked.

I assumed the same yesterday, didn't I?

Jack stepped back up into the hallway, then approached the door in question.

At first he didn't want to touch the door handle. What if when he did, the door swung open and let him inside again? Admitted him in to lie on that bed where he'd dreamt of that strange woman?

He grinned a moment at the sexual memory, his penis growing hard in his shorts. Yeah, that had been one hell of a dream alright.

Then he shook the memory off. His penis stayed hard, as if it wanted him to enter the bedroom, but he ignored it. He wasn't going in there to have another wet dream, if indeed he'd had one in the first place. By now Jack had successfully convinced himself that he'd not ejaculated yesterday. He was a rational man: there hadn't been any evidence, no semen anywhere; which simply meant he'd not come. Open and shut. No need to seek paranormal causes for the obvious.

Still feeling a little nervous, he finally reached out and touched the door handle.

He felt relief when the door didn't budge. Yes, it *was* frigging damn locked. Ha ha! He twisted the handle several times to ensure that it was.

Once convinced that the only way to access this room was to use a crowbar on the door, he descended the stairs to pour himself some cereal.

After breakfast, Jack took a brief walk down through his new neighborhood. He didn't really feel up to walking, but felt some exercise would be good for him.

Like most of the neighborhood driveways, Jack's drive lay diagonal to Maple Lake Road, approaching the road from the south at a 45-degree angle. At the foot of his driveway, he crossed the road and crouched by the water's edge for a while, looking for fish. This activity calmed him, and when he left the lakeshore to walk south along the road again, he was humming contentedly to himself.

Approaching the next house, a blue bungalow with wide white windows, he saw one of the kids who lived there. The smallish blond girl. She was coming to throw something in the trashcan at the foot of their drive. She dumped her garbage, then saw him coming and waited for him to reach her.

"Hello, Mr. Crannson," she greeted when they were face to face.

He grinned back. "Hi there!" he said, then looked apologetic and tapped his forehead. "Sorry, but I've forgotten your name."

"Laney. Laney Springer."

"Pleased to meet you *again*, Laney."

"So, how are you enjoying the neighborhood?" she asked.

"Oh, it's great. Nice and quiet like I need." For a moment he felt bad for yesterday suspecting she and her housemates of breaking into his home and opening up the north bedroom.

"You taking a walk somewhere?" Laney asked brightly.

"Just to the convenience store at the corner. I want to buy the day's papers." Buying the papers had been his final excuse for leaving the house. That and looking for fish in the body of water behind them.

She nodded. Jack figured it was time he moved on. Standing here talking to her was making him feel weak all over again.

He must have winced, because she asked: "Are you alright, Mr. Crannson? You look worn out. I mean, like, really really tired."

Jack forced a smile. "Just overworked." He gestured down the road. "It's been great meeting you again, Laney. I'd better just hurry down the road and buy the papers and get home and back into bed."

She nodded. "Well, see you around then. And if you need any help with fixing up the house, just let us know. Cass is a good handyman; he's great with tools and all that kinda stuff."

Cass? Who's Cass? Jack thought quickly. *Oh, her boyfriend.* If he recalled correctly, the third kid who lived her was her older brother. He couldn't remember that one's name though. Looking behind her, he'd already noticed the two motorbikes parked out front by the garage.

He nodded. "Thanks for the offer, Laney. I'll be in touch if you guys can help me out in any way."

"Bye." She waved and walked back up her driveway.

Jack watched her go for a while.

Nice kid, he thought as he resumed his walk down the road.

***

Back home with the morning papers, Jack quickly realized that taking that walk had been a really bad idea. Once he sat in his chair, he began feeling worse than ever. The weakness hit him with twice the intensity he'd felt while he'd been talking to the neighbor girl Laney.

Good thing I'm back home then.

He decided he'd watch himself carefully today; take a sedative, stay in bed and sleep. If he still felt this bad tomorrow morning, that would most likely mean he'd caught a bug somewhere. He'd skip the office and head for the clinic instead.

He settled back in his chair and read the news. But oh, he felt so tired. Too tired to read even.

Jack soon felt himself drifting off to sleep.

CHAPTER 9

Jack

This time it didn't take long for the dream to claim Jack, wrapping him in its soft seductive claws. In his dream, Jack rose from the chair he was asleep in and walked through the living room to the stairs.

He didn't feel tired anymore. Full of strength and expectation, he climbed the stairs. A brief period followed when the hallway walls seemed to wobble around him, and then he was entering the north bedroom, his feet sliding noiselessly over the floor as the door shut itself behind him.

The bedroom was empty until he crossed the red circle on the floor. And then she was suddenly there again. The woman Cali, as solid as he last recalled her. And as naked as the last time. Beauty personified and so sexy that he wanted to weep at the sight of her.

"Welcome back, Jack," she said, delight in her voice and her eyes. "I'm glad you came. But then, you had no real choice in the matter."

He stood before her in his dream trance, his gaze falling to the floor, then slowly rising up her legs, pausing at the dusky triangle of hair that filled her crotch, then rising further up to her lovely breasts, with their nipples like brown sweets; and finally up to her face. That face with its insanely seductive gaze. Those piercing blue eyes that beamed lust at him like lasers. Those lips that seemed made for kissing.

This time Jack instantly noticed something lurking behind Cali's gestures of seduction. Something in her eyes. Something unpleasant. She wanted something from him. But what?

But then, she cocked a finger at him and stepped back towards the bed. Jack followed her, unable to resist and not wanting to either. His cock was hard and he was aware of slipping off his shorts and tee shirt as he followed her lead.

She lay back and parted her legs wide. He felt like weeping with delight as he stared at her pussy, so pinkly perfect in its surrounding of black hair; her pleasure hole seeming irresistible and moist with her feminine secretions.

She cocked her finger up at him again. "Come inside me, I'm wet with desire for you."

Jack climbed onto the bed and slid between her legs, slipped his penis inside her. Once again . . . oh, shit, he'd forgotten what she felt like down there . . . it felt like he'd been plugged into the mains and insulated from suffering any harm. He felt electrified by her vagina.

She grinned at the shocked delight in his eyes. "With me, it's better each time. Now fuck me. Fuck me very hard and come inside me."

Jack fucked her as hard as he could. He felt like he'd ejaculate at any moment, but that didn't happen. His orgasm was delayed and delayed, while he pumped and sweated on her.

Cali held onto him and gasped and moaned, but even when she came, he felt as if she was going through the motions in some way. Not sexually, her orgasmic throes were genuine enough—either that or she'd been working in porn since her teen years.

But still, in this dream state which forbade dishonesty, Jack sensed that Cali was using him in some way.

Her climax over, she lay back gasping and stroked his face. "Okay, your turn now. Come inside me."

And just like that, as if her words had flicked a switch in his testicles, Jack's orgasm swept up through his crotch. So intense that it was almost painful. Once again he seemed to be ejaculating out his entire scrotum forever and ever.

And when it was over all he could do was lie on Cali in complete exhaustion, while for her own part, she stroked his face and gushed, "Oh, thank you so much, Jack. Thank you, baby. You've no idea how much I needed that from you."

He tried to reply, but was too tired to.

But then, as sometimes happened in dreams, Jack felt miraculously rejuvenated. His manhood was once more stiff and he felt even more sexually energized than he had before they'd done it.

He reached for Cali again. She laughed—he'd forgotten how sexual her laugh was—then parted her thighs for him again. "Yes," she agreed quickly. "Let's do it one more time." And when he once more slid his penis into her, she gasped. "Oh, Jack, you've no idea how wonderful you really are. Oh, baby, you're just the man I've needed all these years."

Jack thrust away happily between her legs. At some point he realized that he was dreaming, that this woman he was making love to didn't exist outside of his imagination, but it didn't matter. What mattered here and now were the sensations he was getting from her, sensations he'd never felt before in his genitals. It didn't even matter that he knew this dream woman was using him for some arcane purpose known only to herself.

CHAPTER 10

Jack . . . Afterwards

Jack woke up slowly. It took him a while to open his eyes, and when he did so he was bothered by his surroundings.

I fell asleep in the living room . . .

He'd remembered that clearly. Only now he was upstairs, in the locked north bedroom and its door was unlocked (he could see down the hallway and into his own open bedroom). In here, the lights were on and he was spread-eagled in the bed. He was also naked. He had no memory of either climbing the stairs or of getting undressed.

In fact, all Jack remembered was the dream. The dream. Exactly the same as the last time. Himself in bed with Cali. Himself fucking Cali, her body silky against his. Sex with her had been just as fantastic as before. She'd thrilled his body and mind like no other woman ever had.

Once again, Jack felt as sexually satisfied by the dream as if he'd ejaculated for real, but once more, as far as he could see, there was no semen anywhere on his body or the bed covers.

He lay there sated yet bothered. The sensation of his dream lover hadn't yet left him. Jack could almost feel her breasts and thighs still pressed against him.

Wow, Cali was great in bed. Jack easily admitted that not even his wife Samantha came close in the sexual department. But that was of course to be expected. Sam was real life, Cali was fantasy; and fantasy was always better than the real thing.

And, as Jack saw it, the responsibility for his creating 'Cali' rested entirely on Samantha's pretty shoulders. If she'd only been around when he needed her . . .

He grinned, then said aloud: "Wow, Jack Crannson, you've definitely gotten yourself into a thing this time."

He didn't understand it, of course. Had he sleepwalked up here? That was the only rational explanation that came to his mind. He tried to sit up, to get a good view of the door. Was the key in the lock? If it was, that would mean he'd unlocked the door himself. Which would support the sleepwalking explanation for his being in here.

Now, he found he was almost too tired to move.

"Damn!" he groaned. "What the hell's going on here?" If he'd been tired before, now he felt almost dead. He felt like he'd been set on by leeches.

It's these sexual dreams, he quickly realized. *Each time I dream of Cali I wake up like this. But why?*

Why? He didn't know why.

And he couldn't ponder that oddity too long either. He'd just become aware of yet another oddity:

The bedroom was suffused by a red glow. This additional light was coming from the floor. Jack realized that during his attempt to sit up, he'd noticed something red out of the corner of his eye. He remembered the red circle on the floor. But was it glowing?

Summoning all his strength, Jack finally did sit up.

Yes, the red circle on the floor *was* glowing. It appeared to be fluorescent, like a neon circle in the floor.

Jack felt really worried now. He clearly remembered what old Mr. Bannering had told him about this room. "Keep it shut, son! Don't you ever go in there!" Advice he'd dismissed as senile raving. But what if Mr. Bannering's warning hadn't been just an old man's superstitions, or obsessive displaced memories copied from a film he'd once watched. What if . . . ?

Jack considered: *The first time I entered here. I didn't notice this red ring at all . . . then I came back during the storm, and after my dream it was here; just not very bright . . . and now . . . now . . .*

He regarded the red circle with some dread. Then, still undecided what to make of it, he looked around the room. Everything else seemed normal enough. (Not that there was anything in here other than the furniture and shut drapes anyway.) But the red glow on the floor, tinting as it did the lower half of the room pink, created its own oddity.

Jack considered the puzzle for a short while longer, then painfully hauled himself up off the old bed and made the long trek down the hallway to his own bedroom.

This time he didn't bother locking the north door behind him. While stepping over its threshold he'd noticed the key in the lock. He figured if he was that desperate to have dream sex with a figment of his imagination, so be it.

Oh, if it just wasn't so tiring. I feel like death warmed over.

He did turn around once to stare at the red ring on the bedroom floor.

Yes, the ring was still there, as inexplicable as before.

"I'll have to get someone in to have a look at that," he muttered to himself. "Maybe that's synthetic wood and there's a neon ring down there. A prop for some kinky sex show? Or why else is that bed positioned right in the center of it?"

Then he remembered his wife had promised to call him today. He paused at the top of the stairs. His phone was downstairs in the living room.

Has Sam called already? Is she pissed off with me again? Do I need to call a doctor? What the hell time is it anyway? Is this even still Sunday?

He decided he didn't have enough strength to make it down the stairs and back up again.

That decided and with no answers to his questions, Jack resumed his trudge to his bedroom. Once safely there, he dropped into his own bed and fell stone asleep.

CHAPTER 11

Caspar, Dray, & Laney

"Aw, dude, come on," Dray said. "No way that that happened to you." Beer in hand, Dray was sitting on the living room floor, his PlayStation video war-game paused for the moment.

Caspar rolled his eyes, then leaned forward on the sofa. He'd expected this. "Look . . . man, do you think I'll lie to you? Think on this: have I ever lied to you about anything?"

Dray poked a finger into his cheek, stared at the ceiling and made a ponderous face. "Well there was that time in eight grade when Miss . . . . Miss . . . man, what was her name again? The redhead with the glasses and the big boobs?"

"I mean, have I ever lied to you about anything *serious*?"

Dray shook his head. "No, you haven't." Then his eyes widened in shock. "Dude, are you frigging *serious* that this happened last night? A naked chick outside Bannering's place?"

Caspar shook his head, then turned to Laney. "I think he's missing the point of my story."

Laney shifted on her chair and nodded. "Yeah." She rolled her eyes and waved at her brother. "Duh? The issue here isn't that the slut didn't have clothes on, but that she *vanished*. You know like, in she went 'Poof!' in the night air."

"You believe me then?" Caspar asked Laney.

She looked confused. "I don't know. I know you're serious and that you wouldn't make something like that up . . ." then her eyes lit up as a thought crossed her mind and she scowled at Caspar. "Oh, oh . . . so *that's why* you were so boned up last night? It was that slut, not me? She's the one who got you that hard? Shit, you sleazy guys are all alike! Once you get a gape at some tits you lose your damn minds. Shit—I should have known it was something nasty like that, the way you were all over me like glue."

Caspar was saved from replying by Dray, who asked, "Er, little sister, . . . at what point did we stop discussing your boyfriend's weird experience and start talking about porn?"

Laney gave him the finger. "Go jerk off, bro. You're long overdue to lose your cherry."

Dray rolled his eyes. "Laney, I've told you time and again that I'm not a damn virgin. What's the matter with you anyway?"

This time it was Caspar who came to Dray's rescue and defused what would certainly have degenerated into mudslinging sibling rivalry. "Guys, don't get sidetracked here, alright? Stay with me here . . . please."

"Oh, alright," Laney agreed. "But you gotta promise to take me clubbing next weekend as payment for last night's BS that you pulled."

Caspar readily agreed. It was a trifling price to pay for peace with the girl he loved. He looked at Dray. Dray looked reluctant to let the slight die. Caspar knew why: it was true—Dray Springer *was* still a virgin at age 20. In this modern day and age, an embarrassing admission to make except for one who was studying to be a priest. Yes, Dray was overweight, but that wasn't his problem. Lots of girls found him cute. Dray was just too painfully shy to make anything out of the romantic opportunities that came his way. Caspar was always counselling his best friend to be more proactive about his love life, but no, Dray locked up each time a young woman so much as smiled at him.

And whenever they had an argument, Laney rubbed it in his face. It wasn't as if she was overly 'experienced' herself (Caspar was only her second boyfriend), but at least she wasn't 'saving herself for marriage,' like she often accused her older brother of doing. Of course, like most women in love with their boyfriends, Laney would be more than delighted if Caspar, the current man in her life, turned out to be the 'final' man in her life; she loved him enough to marry him.

He'd assured her he felt the same way about her.

"C'mon, man," Caspar urged his friend. "Cut her some slack for today. I really need to figure this whole thing out."

Dray relented. "Oh, alright." Then he pointed at Laney. "Only, if you call me a virgin one more time, I'll cut Cass's balls off so you never get laid again. Ha ha ha!"

"Ha ha ha? You sound like the baddie in one of your dumb video games." Laney looked like she'd say more, but a pleading look from Caspar stopped her.

"They're my balls, not yours," he said.

Once certain that brother and sister wouldn't start bickering again, Caspar said, "So, guys, this is the thing. You two figure this out for me: did I or didn't I see a naked woman in Mr. Crannson's driveway last night, who was flickering and then suddenly vanished?" He looked helplessly from one face to the other and back again. "Or did I hallucinate it all? Or am I simply going nuts?"

"Were you high?" Dray asked, serious now. "Had you had a toke of some weed?"

"Hell no, bro. You know I can't ride my bike when I'm stoned."

"Then we can rule out hallucinations." Dray's eyes suddenly lit up mischievously. "Hey, what if she was a mermaid? And she came out of the lake to seduce Mr. Crannson, and—" He saw the others looking at him narrowly and shook his head. "Nah, forget I even suggested that." Then, staring at Caspar, he asked hopefully: "She didn't happen to have a tail, did she?"

"No."

Dray shrugged, then remembered his beer and took a sip of it. "Okay, so back to what I was earlier saying—dude, you're not hallucinating." Then frowned at his sister. "Or do you see it differently?"

Laney shook her head. "It's definitely not hallucinations, that's for sure." She scratched her left thigh and then went on: "Dray, do you remember what Kate said when she visited for Christmas?"

"Kate? Who's Kate?" Caspar asked.

Dray crumpled his beer can and dropped it. "Kate Harris. She was old man Bannering's granddaughter. She visited the old guy two Christmases ago—before you moved in with us." He grinned at a memory. "Real pretty girl, though her boobs were on the small side."

"She liked you," Laney said. "She really liked you, man. And you were too chicken to take what she offered."

Caspar hoped they wouldn't resume hostilities. To his relief, Dray shrugged it off. "Yeah, yeah. Well it just didn't work out with her."

"It never does."

Dray waved this comment off too. Then he stared seriously at Caspar. "What's she's referring to are the stories Katie told us about her granddad and the house Mr. Crannson just bought off him."

"What kinda stories?"

Laney shrugged. "The creepy kind. Gramps was apparently scared of something in the north bedroom, that he feared would get out."

Caspar leaned forward. "What kind of a 'something?' Did she have any idea what was supposed to be locked up in the room?"

Dray shook his head while opening a fresh can of beer. "Nah, she didn't say. I don't think she knew herself. She thought—"

"No, no—she *did* say," Laney interrupted. "Kate said it was some kind of evil essence. Something her granddad had either trapped in their or inherited. There was a bed involved." She looked confused for a moment. "Though I didn't get that part at all."

"Yeah, now I remember," Dray agreed. "Something about a spirit trapped in a bed, which would wreak hell if released."

Caspar sighed. "A spirit trapped in a bed? That sounds crazier than what I saw."

"What if that's *what* you saw?" Dray asked.

Laney shook her head. "How would he see it—the spirit—if it's trapped in the bed?"

"Good question," Caspar agreed with her. "There is one other question though: did Kate Harris say how the spirit was supposed to be released?"

Dray laughed. "Dude, you're really taking this shit seriously. Maybe too seriously."

Caspar sighed. "If you'd been with me last night . . ." He returned his attention to Laney. "So, did the girl know how the spirit could be set free?"

Laney nodded. "If I remember right, she said you had to sleep in the bed and then the spirit—weird thing is that the spirit was supposed to be female—she'd visit you and have sex with you. Something like that."

Dray burped. "Oh boy—what I wouldn't give for a bed like that."

Laney shot him a hard look, then went on: "We both thought the old guy was just crazy and superstitious, of course, but . . . but Kate said he took it very seriously."

"For real?"

Laney nodded again. "Yeah, old Mr. Bannering was dead serious about no one entering that room. In fact, according to Kate, the bedroom's been locked for the past forty years."

Caspar looked shocked. "Forty years?"

"Yeah," Laney confirmed. "Forty years. Apparently, he shut the room up when her mother was a teenager and never opened it up since."

"Guys," Caspar said quietly, "this is becoming bothering. Just reason along with me. If old Mr. Bannering was so serious about that room not being opened for that long . . . it definitely sounds like more than just a crank tale, right?"

Dray swallowed some more beer. When he lowered the can he looked worried. "Dude, I don't like where this story seems headed. 'Cos what you're suggesting is that the new owner of the house next door—Mr. Crannson—may have unknowingly released what Mr. Bannering had been keeping in check for the past four decades?"

Laney shrugged, then stood up and stretched. "Makes sense though, bro, if all he needs to do to free it is open the bedroom door and sleep in the bed."

Caspar got up too. "Yeah, yeah. But, guys, if that were really the case, wouldn't Mr. Bannering have warned him 'bout not sleeping in there?"

Dray's brow creased up for a moment as he put his brain to work. "Maybe not, If he just wanted to sell the place fast. I remember Kate told us that her parents had been pressurizing him to offload the house on someone and come down south to get a tan on the beaches. So there's the chance he didn't tell Mr. Crannson anything."

"That doesn't really sound like Mr. Bannering," Caspar countered. "He was always such a nice old fellow. Not the sort to send you up Shit Creek without a paddle."

"So maybe he did tell Mr. Crannson the danger," Laney agreed. "But, guys, of course, if he did tell Mr. Crannson that his house had a haunted bedroom, there's no chance in hell of Mr. Crannson believing him."

"Yeah," Dray said philosophically. "How fucked up is that for you?"

"Yeah," Caspar agreed.

"I don't know 'bout you two," Laney said, "but I'm dying for a swim." She cocked her head at Caspar. "How 'bout it? We hit the water?"

"Sure thing," Caspar nodded. He was off work today. He looked at Dray. "You coming with us?"

Dray shook his head and jerked a thumb at the TV screen, where a POV rocket launcher waited to blast to smithereens whatever hapless enemy emerged around the end of the digital wall just ahead of it. "I've gotta finish this damn game. And then I've got second shift to make." Then he grinned, and made a phone sign at his ear with thumb and pinky finger. "But, make certain to call me if you see your spooky woman skinny dipping."

"In your dreams," Laney said, giving him the finger.

CHAPTER 12

Jack

Monday morning. The bedside alarm rang. Jack woke up slowly. Then he sat up carefully, watching to see how he felt today.

Not too bad, but yet not good. He didn't feel as drained as yesterday, but still, when he touched his body, his skin had a raspy unnatural feel to it and also felt less firm than usual.

He sat there revisiting yesterday in his mind.

***

Jack had no idea how long he'd slept in the north room before moving to his own bed, but when he'd finally woken up a second time, it was four in the evening. Most of the day was over. He'd been able to get out of bed then. He'd had a shower to wake himself up, then gone downstairs and made himself a chicken and lettuce sandwich. No more booze. For all he knew, yesterday's early alcohol intake may have played an integral part in his weakness. Instead, he'd made himself a mug of very strong coffee.

While eating, he'd checked his phone. Five missed calls, none from Samantha. Two voicemails. Neither from Samantha either. She'd disappointed him again.

Both voicemails and three of the calls came from Rich Rogers of Quantum Excavating, concerning road specifications for the Melas shopping center his architecture firm was currently handling. Rich was having trouble with the Department of Highways getting a permit to make the entrance to the property from the main road. They apparently had an older version of the plans and those older plans didn't provide enough of a visual for oncoming traffic not to be dangerous.

He'd called Rich back, told him what to do, and also told he might not be into work on Monday, though he wasn't yet certain. Janice or Gary had the plans for the building that was to be constructed on the site, but could get Mr. Rogers what he needed for the permit if necessary. Hopefully he could count on at least one of them to keep things running smoothly between Rich and the Department of Highways, and not screw things up further.

The other two calls were from Robin Thurgood, a good friend of Samantha's who lived in Bridgeport. He'd called her back. She'd just wanted to say hello. She'd heard (meaning Samantha had told her) that he'd moved down from Cheat Lake to Maple Lake and wondered if she could come visit.

"Sam told me the place looks great inside, and that you've got this fantastic waterside view. I just can't wait to see it!" she'd said enthusiastically.

Jack had begged off for this weekend. "I'm too tired—like I caught the flu or something. But is next weekend alright for you? Work permitting, of course."

"Sure, it is," Robin had replied.

She'd sounded disappointed though. Jack suspected Samantha wanted Robin to keep an eye on him for her, to ensure he wasn't keeping a mistress in the house. Robin was a bit nosy and liked such intrigues. He could just imagine the two of them conversing about him, insinuating all kinds of nonsense about male infidelity.

After Robin hung up, Jack had made himself another sandwich and another mug of strong coffee. He'd watched TV for a while, a live baseball game. This time, although he was still weak, the strong coffee meant he hadn't dozed off.

It hadn't taken long, however, before the weird puzzle of his sleepwalking returned to haunt him. He had too many unanswered questions, the most bothering being that of the crimson ring on the bedroom floor.

Halfway through the baseball game, he'd gotten up and climbed the stairs again.

The north bedroom door was still open; the key still in its lock. Jack had peered inside once, noted that the ruby circle still glowed all around the bed, then had switched off the bedroom lights. The effect of his doing so had been both startling and frightening. With the red circle now its only light source, the bedroom looked like a demon's cavern. Jack had stared at the bed, blinking his eyes when, for a moment, there seemed to be a naked woman lying on it. Cali? He'd also imagined he'd heard faint, mocking laughter. But of course, there'd been no one there. The illusion of a woman had merely been the product of his over-expectant mind. The vision's accompanying sounds were most likely distant thunderclouds threatening a return of the rain.

He'd locked the door and returned the key to the nightstand drawer.

***

Now, Jack got up and shambled into the bathroom to urinate. He'd already decided he couldn't make it to work today. He'd go to the clinic and have some tests run on him. It was very possible that he'd inverted cause and effect: that it was the weakness making him dream and not the dreams making him weak.

So, maybe I have caught a bug after all, he thought, stepping up to the toilet. He had no doubt that something was wrong though.

In any event, the office would survive a day without him. He finished peeing, flushed, then stepped up to the mirror to stare at his reflection.

It was now that Jack got his first shock of the day.

He seemed to have aged overnight. He was thirty-eight, but his face looked at least ten years older.

This isn't me, he thought in horror, reaching up a hand and tugging on the slack sagging skin. "This isn't me," he said aloud. "No, it's not."

But then reality set in and he examined himself in more detail. The most convincing detail came from the skin of his neck, which now hung loose. Jack tugged on the loose flesh, then examined his chest. He'd never been muscular, but now he looked 'slack.'

Like I've withered a little. Like I've . . . I don't look older, I look emaciated, like I'm starving!

The weakness returned then, along with a spell of dizziness that made the bathroom reel around him. To prevent himself falling, he grabbed the sink, then shut his eyes tight until he felt strong enough to open them again.

Then he made his way back into the bedroom and fell flat on the bed.

The only thought in Jack's mind now was to get to a hospital.

Five minutes later, he felt strong enough to use the phone. First he called his office and told his secretary he wouldn't be in today, and to have Gary call him at home for instructions once he got in.

Jack was next about to dial 911, when logically or illogically, he changed his mind about doing so. Though he clearly wasn't able to drive in his present state, he didn't seem to be in any immediate danger of dying.

So, instead of Emergency Services, Jack called Samantha. As usual, her number went right to voicemail. He left a message telling her he wasn't fine and he needed her to come take him to the hospital. Then, just for good measure, he sent her both a Facebook IM and text message saying the same thing.

He lay back in bed, thinking over what he'd just done. At best, it was childish trying to get Samantha's attention this way; at worst, it might prove to be suicidal. Supposing what was wrong with him killed him before she decided to listen to her voicemails or check her messages?

But then, suddenly, Jack he had more to worry about than either his wife thinking him childish or his dying from his strange affliction.

All of a sudden noises were coming from outside Jack's bedroom. The bedroom door was shut so he couldn't see down the hallway, but he was sure the noises were coming from the north bedroom.

Jack felt intense alarm at this extraordinary situation. As with the first time he'd heard similar noises from that part of his new house, now again he wondered if he really shouldn't just call the police and let them handle things. Once more, his final conclusion was the same: the problem was that it was such an irrational situation. What if the cops arrived and just like before, the room was empty, again.

And with me looking like I'm on a drug jag!

Once more, he had to handle this himself. With misgivings, Jack got his gun out from under his pillow.

Once he opened his bedroom door, he saw clearly that something was wrong. The north door was open again. It wasn't banging shut like the previous time, so there was no way for him to know what was making the noise.

"Maybe this time the dresser's jumping up and down, or the bed," he grumbled. "Shit. I can't believe Bannering sold me a house with a damn poltergeist in it. At the very least he could have warned me about the damn thing."

A strange thought for a man who didn't believe in ghosts.

Also, seeing as he'd left the lights off in the north bedroom, that surreal red glow from yesterday was spilling out through the open door. And if anything, the crimson light seemed more intense than it had yesterday.

The mysterious noise from the bedroom continued. Jack made his slow, tired way to the waiting door.

Then he paused inside the opening and stared. And stared. And stared.

Of what had been making the noise, Jack saw no sign. But there was a naked woman standing beside the bed. She was inside the red circle. The red circle which now blazed as if the bedroom floor was on fire.

It was Cali . . . and Jack didn't doubt that this time she was here for real, in the flesh. Cali, exactly as she'd been in his dream. Black hair, Junoesque body, lovely face . . .

She smiled on seeing him. "Hello, Jack."

How . . . what . . . where . . . ? The questions flooded into his mind. He stared at her as she crossed the blazing red circle and came towards him.

She was incredible: lovely, stupendous, fantastic, a total joy to behold. A body impossible to resist and eyes that beamed sexual invitation at him. Those large, perfectly curved breasts; stiff nipples that indicated her own arousal.

Despite his tiredness, the sight of her made his cock stiffen.

"You don't know how long it's been since I've left that damn ring, Jack," she said. "I've much to thank you for."

Her tinkling voice kept Jack's penis hard. He was confused and scared at this fresh impossible happening in his life and yet he had an erection, which wouldn't go down. His cock visibly pushed out the front of his pajama pants.

She was still smiling at him. And now, just like in his last dream vision of her, he read a dark intent in her eyes. This intent that had little or nothing to do with sexual lust. Yes, Cali desired sex with him, but this wasn't because she desired 'him,' as such. She wanted him because she wanted something he had. He was a means to an end.

And he also read in Cali's eyes that though she looked nice, her intentions were bad. Really evil. Her beautiful gaze revealed an intense cruelty in her; spitefulness mingled with an ambition that wouldn't be thwarted.

That was as far as Jack's thoughts got. Because, the next moment Cali reached him and slipped her arms around him. Her body pressed against his, and he gave up his ruminations on how evil she was, abandoning them in the whirlwind of sheer pleasure that her touch gave him.

"Thank you, Jack," she whispered and pressed her lips to his.

She kissed him. And when she did so, his endurance ceased. His strength finally gave out and he fainted in her arms.

***

When Jack revived again, he was still in the north bedroom. He was lying on the bed. He was naked again and Cali was sucking on his penis.

He lay there motionless. He wanted to push her off him, but his hands refused to move. Her mouth felt incredible on his erection, but he was scared of its implications.

As Cali fellated him he felt a part of himself leave him and enter her. In the dream he'd not felt this happen, but then seeing as it was a dream, maybe he had felt such a sensation, but in the midst of the electricity sparked by the frantic sexual coupling, he'd not paid it any notice. Either way, this was an awful new sensation for Jack. He couldn't describe it; He wasn't dissolving and yet it felt as if he was. His strength was somehow transferring itself to this woman. Now his prematurely aged and withered reflection in the mirror made sense to him. Cali was leeching him.

"Please!" he gasped. "Stop."

Her lips plopped wetly off his cock. She raised her head and stared at him. "No," she replied simply. "I'm rewarding you for what you've done for me. Relax. You'll really enjoy this."

"No!" Jack gasped, but her lips had already fastened around the head of his penis again and the pleasure she offered him once more coursed through his body. He lay there, the delicious sensations mesmerizing him. Then he came into her mouth. He squirted out his semen in wet jets and heard Cali lustily and noisily gulping it down.

And while ejaculating, he felt more of 'himself' leaving him and entering her.

Oh, dammit, he thought glumly, *next time I stare in the mirror, I'm gonna look fifty years old; shrunken like a goddamned stick insect.*

Cali lifted her head from Jack's penis and licked her lips clean. She smiled at him. "Did you enjoy that, Jack?"

"You're killing me. How can I enjoy dying?"

She shrugged as if displeased by his criticism of her. "Well, I liked it anyway. And I'm *not* hurting you, Jack. Well, not really. Not as much as I could if I chose to."

He found sufficient energy to raise himself up on the pillows. "Why the hell am I so damn weak then?"

She sat beside him and roved her fingers through his chest hair. "I'm a succubus. I feed on human energy," she explained. "If it stops, I stop too—I'll fade back into the bed." She regarded him with a cold smile. "Being female, I eat male energy. Sometimes I even kill those I sleep with. But . . . I like you, Jack," she said, stroking his cheek. "I really do. And so I won't kill you. You'll live here with me. I'll take a little life from you occasionally, but you'll be my true love. Alright, Jack?"

He nodded weakly; he already knew she didn't like him at all. It was written all over her face. She was merely using him as a means to an end—whatever that end might be. He had the sudden understanding that at the moment Cali needed him—he was essential to her nasty plans in some way—but his usefulness might soon pass and then he'd be just one orgasm away from extinction. Because (and this was one of the things that scared him about her), while she'd been fellating him he'd sensed that she was holding back from draining him, that if she really wanted to she could empty him like he was a bottle of Coca-Cola.

"Okay, alright," he cautiously replied her, knowing that for the moment his wellbeing rested in her hands. "But, I don't believe any of this is really happening to me. A succubus? Aren't succubuses supposed to haunt dreams?"

She laughed nastily and tapped his belly with a sharp fingernail. "Surely you can answer that one yourself? Where did you first meet me? At the shopping mall? Swimming in the lake outside?"

He conceded she was right; yes, she had been in his dreams. But now?

"Yeah?" he asked, not concealing his confusion. "And what are you doing outside of my dreams then? Or better yet, what the hell is a succubus doing here in the first place?"

"You bought the house. I come with the house. With this bed actually."

She'd stressed 'come' as if she meant the sexual climax version of the word.

Jack pointed down at the red ring on the floor, the glow of which had dimmed somewhat since he'd woken up. "And this? What does this ring mean?"

Now Cali looked angry. "An enemy put that there to stop me leaving this room. After you and I had sex here that first time, I tested the ring's restraints—I projected myself outside this room, down your driveway to the road, but the bed jerked me back inside here again. Clearly, I wasn't strong enough to leave yet."

Jack felt some relief. It was one thing to find a naked woman in your house whom you'd only previously met in your dreams, and who might be able to fuck you to death; but clearly another to discover she at least had some restrictions on her movements.

His hopes of keeping Cali in this bedroom were however instantly shattered:

"So after that I knew I needed more energy. So I brought you back upstairs to have sex with me again. And now, the restraints are off for good. Yes, Jack, my love—since you've fed me, I'm now free again."

She stretched her gorgeous body, then her lovely face creased into a frown. "I'm just so delighted to finally get out of here. Forty years. Imagine that, Jack—forty long years of miserable captivity. Locked here in this bedroom—in this damn bed—by that crazy old man. I'm of a mind to take out my frustrations on everyone." She grinned evilly and patted his cheek. "Not on you, of course. You, Jack, are very special to me. I could never do a thing to hurt you. Never. But everyone else . . ."

Cali said a whole lot of similar things. Jack, unable to raise even his little finger from the draining she'd just giving him, listened to her talk. In rising horror he realized his life had just become really complicated.

CHAPTER 13

Jack & Cali

"I want to visit the town," Cali said.

Jack nodded. "Alright, I'll see you later." To his mind, this presented a great opportunity to escape. Each moment spent with Cali convinced him the more that he was in danger. Jack didn't need much convincing anyway; the way he felt was sufficient warning of his peril. So, once she left the house, so was he. He'd be out of here like a flash . . . Screw waiting for Samantha—he'll call an ambulance. From the hospital he'd ask his secretary Janice to arrange to collect his things from the house. He'd not dispatch her alone though; that would likely be dangerous. No, he'd ask Gary to accompany her. As for the house? Well, Cali could keep it.

Jack and Cali were now in *his* bedroom. Demonstrating superhuman strength, she'd practically carried him from the north bedroom to this south one. During that short trip along the hallway, though his feet touched the floor on occasion as he staggered along at Cali's side, Jack had had the impression that he was floating.

"Oh, this is real nice," Cali had said on seeing Jack's bedroom. "I'll sleep in here from now on. "You can have my room and bed."

Now, seated at the foot of the bed and regarding Jack, who lay stretched out on his back, exhausted and gasping for breath like a fish out of water, Cali said, "I'm not visiting the town alone. You're coming with me." They were both still naked. Jack was covered with the sweat of their last sexual encounter; Cali looked cool as frost.

On hearing what she'd just said, Jack's hopes fell. "Come on, lady. I'm too tired to go anywhere now." He weakly gestured to the dresser. "Look, there's my car keys. Take the SUV. I'm sure to still be here when you get back, right?"

She frowned and shook her head. "What's an SUV?"

"It's a large type of car. Mine's parked downstairs."

"I can't drive, Jack. You'll drive me to town and back."

He stared at her in some confusion. Didn't she notice the obvious? "Cali," he wheezed, "you've completely worn me out with all that fucking. I can't even get out of bed, I'm a candidate for the ER." His voice rose in anger and confusion. "How in the hell am I supposed to drive a car in this goddamn condition you've put me in?"

"You will," she said easily. "I'll fix you when we're ready to leave. She pointed to the wardrobe. "You're wearing a wedding ring, meaning you're married. Are any of your wife's clothes in there?"

Jack tried to bluff her. "You're right—I am married. My wife's a private eye; she's very tough and she's due back any minute now." He tried to look concerned. "I really like you, Cali, I don't want to see you get hurt. It's best you leave now before Sam gets home."

Cali laughed. "I don't think she'll be back any time soon, Jack. Oh, she's tough, is she?" She laughed even louder. "Well, so am I, honey." With that, her left hand, which she'd been pointing at the wardrobe, suddenly altered into a large black claw with long talons. She waved the claw at him. "See, Jack? Your little woman won't stand a chance of survival if she gets in my way." For emphasis, she dropped her claw to his left thigh and dug it into his skin.

"Yeow!" Jack howled. "Stop it! Stop it!"

Cali dragged the claw down Jack's thigh for two inches, leaving a line of blood. Then laughing, she converted the claw back into her hand again. "Do you understand, Jack? I don't play games. I'm not playing with you right now. I'm not fucking human, make certain that you get that. I want what I want and you're going to help me get it. I have aims and desires, and you're going to help me achieve them. Do you understand?" She grinned, which made her look both more evil and more beautiful, then ran her index finger through the blood welling from his thigh and lifted the bloody finger for him to see. "Or . . . do you want me to demonstrate my seriousness on your other leg as well?"

He shook his head quickly. "No, no no! I'll do whatever you say! Just don't cut me again!"

She grinned. Jack expected her to suck his blood off her finger like a vampire would. But she didn't. She wiped the finger clean on his thigh. "So now, back to what I asked you: are there women's clothes in the wardrobe?"

"Yes," Jack groaned. "Sam's pants and tops are in the right side, at the far right. She left them here the last time she visited me. She—"

Too late, Jack realized what he'd just said. "What I meant was, er . . ."

Cali, however, had already noted his slip-of-tongue. "So your wife *visits* you? Meaning she doesn't live here? That's very convenient for me."

She got up off the bed and crossed to the wardrobe. This was to the right of the bed, beside the bathroom door, and was built in three sections. As per Jack's description, Samantha's clothes were hung at the far right edge of the closet. They weren't many—two sets of pants, a denim skirt, three or four tops and a blue satin party dress. Cali examined the clothes, finally settling on the denim skirt and a white tank top. She pulled those on. While she dressed he stared at her ass, uncertain what it was about her that—despite his now being utterly terrified of her—still turned him on. His thigh hurt badly where she'd cut him, but in spite of that, his penis threatened another erection. He desperately thought against getting hard, instinctively knowing that if Cali saw him erect, she'd insist on having sex one more time, with the result of him losing even more of himself to her than he already had.

And . . . *Oh, shit! How the hell could I frigging slip up like that and let her know that Sam doesn't live here with me?*

Cali finished dressing. She checked out her appearance in the mirror for a minute or so, then turned to stare coldly at Jack. "Your wife's shoes?"

"Same place, right at the bottom. I think there's two pairs there." He had to admit that she looked gorgeous in Samantha's clothes. The skirt and top both hugged her body. And she did have much larger breasts than Samantha anyway. Once again, her nipples seemed erect, pushing against the shirt, which seemed about to burst from the effort of containing her breasts.

Cali searched the bottom of the wardrobe for the shoes. Samantha had left three pairs there. Cali settled on a pair of brown sandals. She slipped these on and turned to face Jack. "How do I look?"

"Great, fucking fantastic," he replied honestly.

She nodded, pleased by his compliment. "Did she leave any makeup?"

He shook his head."

She shrugged, then said, "Alright, time for you to get ready too." She crossed over to the bed and, with a queer look in her eyes, lightly touched Jack's forehead. He felt a gently buzzing go through him, and then suddenly, he felt strong again.

I'm getting out of here, he immediately thought. *I'll fake her along, but once we get outside, I'm legging it to the road and flagging down whoever's coming!*

But even as he thought this, Jack realized it wasn't going to happen. Yes, Cali's touch had energized him, but it had also put her in control of his mind. He felt her governance settle over his brain like an iron fist enclosing a tomato. And just like that simile, he realized too that if he dared disobey her, she could pulp his mind with agony.

In horror, Jack Crannson realized that from now on he'd be forced to do whatever this demon woman wanted him to.

"I see that you understand," Cali told him. "I really like you, Jack. Just do what I say and you'll have no problems at all. But if you don't . . ." She let the threat hang.

"I will," Jack quickly agreed, defeated for the moment. "I will."

She smiled at him. "Alright then. Get out of bed and get dressed. Have a bath first if you like. Then you'll drive me into Bridgeport. I want to see how the place has changed in the past forty years."

CHAPTER 14

Jack & Cali

"I can't really leave the house for any appreciable length of time," Cali told Jack as he drove the silver Kia Sorento SUV along the highway. "It's dangerous for me. So for now, this will be my only such sojourn. But I intend to enjoy myself this once."

"Where would you like us to go?" Jack asked her, turning the vehicle onto Interstate 79. Wanting to avoid driving past his office in case someone noticed them, he'd taken a circuitous route around town, driving round the outskirts of Bridgeport and entering it from the south.

"Oh, anywhere nice," she replied airily, sitting legs crossed and relaxed beside him in the front passenger seat. "And when we get back to the house, I'd like to spend some time out by the lake."

He nodded, committed to keeping her sweet. Her mental control hung in his head like a hammer, iron fingers cradling his brain. He found it impossible to contradict her. Whatever Cali wanted automatically became what he wanted too. He just hoped she'd not suggest doing something unreasonable, such as insisting they make love in the middle of the road. Because if she did, he'd certainly want to do it too.

But to his relief, she didn't. She seemed satisfied to simply be free again, staring at everything they passed as if it was the most incredible thing in existence. Jack almost felt for her. Forty years was a hell of a long time to be chained in one place.

So they drove on. Occasionally, she'd tell him to park the car. He'd park and she'd get out and stare at storefront windows with all the wonderment of an alien visiting Earth for the first time.

On his own part, he continued to feel energized, but had no idea how long this burst of strength would last.

It wasn't entirely bad, however. Being with such a beautiful woman did something for a man's sense of positivity. Jack couldn't help but feel a little proud at the looks Cali kept getting from people each time she left the car to window-shop. Once he even caught himself grinning when she walked past a group of workmen repairing a hole on Main Street. The men wolf-whistled after her; several of them appeared struck dumb by her beauty. For her part, appreciating the male lust she'd generated, Cali smiled sweetly back at them and swayed her hips more devastating than a catwalk model.

But then, as she climbed back into his SUV, Jack groaned at the irony of it: *Oh, if those guys only knew the shit I'm in right now, they'd flee for their damn lives.*

While with the succubus on this sightseeing tour to reacquaint herself with Bridgeport, Jack made a point of behaving himself. He was aware that she didn't trust him not to attempt to make a break for freedom. But, as he'd earlier resolved to do, he played it safe, controlling himself on the couple of occasions when she got lost from his sight in a crowd and he might have driven off and left her behind. He didn't know how far her hold over his mind extended and didn't dare try to find out. His thigh still hurt from where she'd clawed it. He didn't want her hurting him again.

They drove back and forth through Bridgeport for an hour, with Cali's excitement never seeming to diminish, no matter how many times she saw the same things over and over again.

Then, coming up East Main Street for the fifth time that day, Jack told Cali, "Look, let's stop at that coffee shop over there, the one right beside Domino's Pizza. I need to eat some breakfast." He checked his watch. It was a quarter past one. "I mean, some lunch."

He thought she'd refuse his request, but she didn't. "Alright," she agreed. "But don't try any smartness with me. You know what'll happen if you do."

"Sure, sure," he agreed, turning the car off the highway into the Almost Heaven coffee shop's parking lot.

CHAPTER 15

Caspar, Dray, & Laney

Caspar, Dray, and Laney were standing in the parking lot of the Domino's Pizza place on East Main Street when the Silver Kia Sorento SUV pulled up outside the coffee shop next door. Domino's and Almost Heaven Coffees shared a single building.

At first none of the trio noticed the arriving car. Dray had just returned from a pizza delivery, and Caspar was about to set off on one. Laney was with them because she wanted to buy some shoes at the Meadowbrook Mall nearby. Then she'd either hang around Domino's till her bother and her boyfriend finished their shifts or Uber a ride home.

But then Caspar looked sideways and saw the silver SUV.

"Hey—that's her," he said excitedly.

The others stared at him, then followed the direction of his pointing finger.

"Who?" Laney asked.

"The lady I saw who vanished. That's her over there with Mr. Crannson."

The others stared down towards the coffee shop, at the woman standing beside their next door neighbor. Tallish, pretty, long black hair.

Dray whistled. "Well she sure as hell is hot as hell. Is that some body on her or what?"

Laney rolled her eyes, then shrugged. "But . . . that settles it then."

"Settles what?" Dray asked.

"The obvious, elder brother. Look—seeing her here proves she's real, not a spook."

Caspar scratched his chin and mused on that. "Yeah. Looks like I was wrong then. But . . . guys I assure you, she *did* disappear."

Laney patted him on the chest. "Sorry, baby, but she *didn't* disappear. All she did was run starkers down the driveway to give you a boner. Which *I* then made disappear."

Caspar nodded. "Yeah, that has to be the case." But his eyes remained troubled.

The couple beside the silver SUV hadn't noticed them; they were talking by the hood of the car.

Laney saw Caspar staring at the woman, a dreamy expression on his face. She prodded him. "Hey, dude, don't you have a job to do?"

Like a diver breaking the surface of swimming pool water, Caspar surfaced from his daze. He got on his motorbike and kicked up the kickstand. "Hey, you guys, I'd better get a move on with this pizza delivery before Mr. Vine fires my ass."

Laney kissed his cheek. "See you later, baby." She waved as he sped the bike out of the parking lot to join the flow of northward traffic along East Main Street.

Laney turned to go inside, then she noticed that Dray was still staring at their neighbor's female companion. She didn't understand he and Caspar's attraction to the woman. Yes, she was pretty, and even from here didn't seem to be wearing a bra to contain her generous chest, but even so . . .

"What's with you?" she asked her brother. "You're acting like you've never seen a slut before. You must have with all that porn you watch."

Dray stood there licking his lips. "Oh man, oh man, oh man. If God would just hear my prayers right now and put me in a bed somewhere with that woman . . . Wow, Laney, just check out those massive boobs! Oh man, Mr. Crannson sure is one lucky guy."

"Yeah, but why does he look so ill?"

"What do you mean, Ill?"

She enunciated the words slowly: "Dray, why does Mr. Crannson look like he should be in the ICU?"

He punched her arm jokingly. "C'mon, Laney, he don't look *that* bad."

She wasn't to be mollified, however. Yes, her comments were partly due to her jealousy because the other woman was so sexy; but Laney also felt she sensed something unpleasant about her.

"Dray—stop thinking with your dick for a moment. Yes, Mr. Crannson does look really ill. He looks much worse than when I saw him on Saturday. In fact, he looks way too ill to be driving around town."

"Maybe she's his nurse?" Dray asked hopefully. The woman and Mr. Crannson were just pushing their way into Almost Heaven Coffees. "Hey, Laney, what'cha think? If she's his nurse, maybe I can find out what hospital she's with and—"

"It's more likely that she gave him whatever sickness he's ill with." Laney tugged on her brother's sleeve. "C'mon, stop gawping at her. Inside. I'm sure they've another delivery ready for you."

He didn't budge. On a whim, Laney looked down at her brother's crotch. She didn't believe it. He had an erection; Dray's cock was visibly pushing against his pants. Just like Caspar said he'd gotten the other night. And she realized she'd not looked at Caspar's crotch before he'd ridden off. Had he had an erection too?

Bothered now, Laney looked back towards the coffee shop. Mr. Crannson and his date were both through the door and out of sight. But, recalling the woman's face, Laney felt uneasy. Something she'd noticed in the woman's face had alarmed her. And no, she didn't think that was merely her jealous imagination.

Then she remembered her brother.

"Aw, Dray," she groaned. "Drayfuss, you've got a damn boner. Get your ass inside before you start wanking in public."

Dray looked down at himself, groaned "Shit!" in disbelief, then covered his erection with his motorbike helmet. He hurried ahead of Laney and vanished into Domino's through the employee's side door.

Laney had the suspicion that he was off to masturbate.

***

Dray *was* off to masturbate. After throwing greetings left and right and explaining he felt really pressed, he dashed into one of the employee toilets, slammed the toilet door shut and quickly unzipped his fly. His penis sprang out like a cobra on the attack. He spat on his palm, and got to work on the stiff erection. As Dray shucked his hand back and forth over his manhood, trying not to grunt and moan, he felt a weird sense of connection with the black-haired woman. He couldn't help it. He felt like she wanted him; all of him; and that if he'd just want her too—if he'd just give himself to her like she wanted him to—that she'd give him sexual pleasure beyond his wildest dreams and imaginings.

The memory of the strange woman with Mr. Crannson had Drayfuss Springer super horny. Oh my good God—her massive breasts dangled before his eyes like fruit he just had to eat.

Dray came in less than a minute, hot jets of his sperm missing the toilet bowl entirely and instead splattering all over the blue toilet seat (which in his haste for relief he'd forgotten to put up).

As Dray ejaculated, his head filled with strange images. He saw himself balling that super-hot lady on a moldy old bed in a red room. The room was red because, while the electric lights were turned off, there was a glowing red circle on the floor around the bed.

The woman was groaning and moaning and having climax after climax, and he was groaning and climaxing too.

The erotic image flickered in and out of Dray's head and then vanished.

He forgot about it. This had been a great orgasm; one of his best ever. As fantastic as when he masturbated to Amy Anderson, his favorite porno star.

Dray stood there shuddering in the toilet. Then, once his breathing settled to normal, he unreeled some toilet paper and after cleaning his hands off, got to work wiping the seat clean.

CHAPTER 16

Cali & Jack

"What do you want?" Jack asked Cali.

"Food and power. I feed on male energy—I need lots of that. And the more I feed, the more power I'll have to control people."

Jack nodded, adding sugar to his coffee. He was having coffee and cake. He stared out of the window at the cars passing by. *I should be at work,* he thought. *We have that Melas reconstruction contract to fulfill, and also the one for the Dodridge County pipeline expansion. I should be overseeing the grand design of buildings, making money, not chauffeuring a succubus around . . .*

He considered their surroundings. There were currently six people in the coffee shop: Jack and Cali, a young couple at a nearby table, and an old gentleman who was sipping coffee and reading the morning paper. The last person was the guy manning the counter—Amos Green. At the moment Amos looked bored. Occasionally, he looked up at the customers, then returned his attention to noting something on his cellphone or menu.

Jack returned his attention to his beautiful companion. "So you plan on eating everyone in town? Don't you think that's overdoing things a bit?" While speaking to her, he kept his voice deliberately low. He already knew the conversation he was having with Cali was crazy; he didn't want the other customers overhearing how crazy it was.

Cali too had a coffee in front of her, but no cake. Black coffee. She raised it and sipped. She made a face. Then she appeared to forget her drink and ponder his question instead. "Not really. I'm a succubus. It's like supernatural prostitution. All I do for a living is fuck sleeping men."

"From what I know about succubae, you're supposed to inhabit dreamland. Alright, even overlooking your weird relationship to that bed, how come you're out here in the human world with me?"

She frowned, then sighed. When she replied, she too spoke softly, though he was uncertain exactly why she was lowering her voice: was she matching her voice to his automatically, or was she simply trying to keep her 'takeover' plans a secret from those present in the shop?

"An unfortunate accident," she explained. "Sometimes things like that happen; one of the unpleasant hazards of being a succubus. Just like with my previous captivities, I'm uncertain exactly what went wrong. One moment I was footloose and free. The next I found myself jailed in that room, attached to that old bed with that red circle drawn around it to prevent me freeing myself. Yes, there I was stuck in the bed with no way back to Hell."

She tried to drink her coffee again, this time with more success. She swirled the mix around in her mouth, swallowed, then added: "So you see—it's not my fault that I'm here and hungry."

Jack saw her point. "Alright, I agree that it's not your fault that you're here in Bridgeport now. But it's not my fault either; and still, you're dragging me into this mess of yours."

"Your fault for buying Bannering's house," Cali said after sipping more coffee. "You could have walked away from the sale. And even after buying the place, you could have left the bedroom door closed."

Jack shook his head at her. "You're a very ungrateful woman." He found his current situation crazy: *Here I am sitting in a coffee shop with a succubus, a vixen from Hell, who's been trapped in a room for forty years. Cali is a demon. . . . and yet . . . and yet, she seems perfectly human.* He looked around the room. Neither the young couple or the old man seemed in anyway bothered by his companion's presence. *Shit! To them we're just another married couple! If she just had horns or a tail!*

The young man at the counter saw Jack looking his way, and gave him an enquiring glance. "You want anything, sir?"

Jack shook his head. "Another coffee maybe, but not right away."

He realized Cali was smiling at him. Her expression was now softer. "Ungrateful? No I'm not, but I can't afford to be sentimental. I'm indebted to you for freeing me—your sperm gave me my initial hardening, but . . . survival comes first. And the only way for me to survive in your physical realm is to feed."

Jack shrugged. "You'll never pull it off anyway. Controlling me, maybe, but not this entire town. Too many people to keep track of."

Now she laughed, though it was Jack's impression that she was also quite angry with him for doubting her. "Oh, you really think so?

Alright, watch this. I'll give you a demonstration of what I can do with my mind when I set my mind to doing it. Just a small demonstration."

"Don't do anything silly."

She smirked back. "Relax, I'm just starting my takeover of Bridgeport."

Jack couldn't relax. He knew she was about to do something fucked-up. He just had no idea how fucked up it would be. He almost expected her to leap up on a table and put on a strip performance. In fact, he wished she'd do that: that would bring the cops, and then hopefully, he could alert someone that something was wrong with him. No, that a whole lot was wrong with him. And of course the police would believe just one thing was wrong with him—that he was crazy. Scratch escaping Cali that way.

"You watching?" Cali asked.

"Yeah," he replied glumly. "Where's your magic trick?"

"Be patient, you'll see. Until I'm stronger it takes a little focus."

Jack waited. Nothing was happening in the coffee shop. Or were zombies going to appear from the walls and eat up everyone?

But no, that didn't happen. The young couple who'd been having lunch were finishing up now, their glazed confectionary demolished to crumbs. The young woman, a blonde professional-looking girl in a blue pantsuit, was sipping her coffee and looking shyly at her companion, while he, a clean-cut banker sort in a gray suit, grinned back loving at her while . . . while . . .

Underneath the table, the young man had his penis out and was masturbating fiercely. His penis was swollen an ugly purple color. The young man glanced sideways at Cali once then returned his attention to his girlfriend, a dreamy grin on his face.

Jack gazed at Cali in horror. She seemed to snap out of a trance, then she smiled back at him. "It took some getting into his mind—he's completely besotted with that silly blonde girl—but . . ."

The couple were seated opposite each other, so the girl had no idea what her boyfriend was up to. Not at first, that was. Meanwhile the old man was still buried in his newspaper and the coffee shop attendant was serving him a fresh coffee. Once the attendant glanced over at Jack and Cali then looked away.

Jack wanted to say something, but had no words. He wanted to yell at the young man to stop masturbating; he wanted to yell at Cali to stop. He said nothing.

Suddenly, the young man began gasping, "Oh, shit, shit!"

His girlfriend immediately leapt to her feet in shock and leaned over the table to see what was going on. Then, both hands over her mouth, she crossed around the table to his side. She stood there staring, then whimpered: "Joey, what the hell are you doing?"

By now, both the old man and the attendant had turned to stare. The coffee shop attendant seemed confused as to what to do. The girlfriend was standing there, looking miserable and trembling like she was having a fit.

Jack grabbed Cali's arm. "Okay, you've made your damn point. Stop it right now!"

"No!"

"Stop it, Joey!" his girlfriend screamed.

"Oh, fuck!" Joey groaned, leaping to his feet. "I feel so good right now!" He picked up his coffee cup and ejaculated into it.

Then—"No, don't! Stop it! Stop it! DON'T!"—the girlfriend screamed, while he emptied the mixture of coffee and semen all over her head.

After pouring the coffee/cum mixture on her, Joey sat down again. He looked confused and lost. His girlfriend stood there looking horrified, with gobs of semen in her hair and both her hair and her blue pantsuit all messed up with dark coffee stains. First, she began crying. Then she grabbed her lunch plate and slammed it down on Joey's head so it shattered. Then she picked up her chair and slammed that too down on Joey's head. The rear of the chair came off. Joey slid from his own chair to the floor with blood streaming from his forehead. He didn't move. His girlfriend stood over him breathing hard, an enraged look on her face.

Jack stared at Cali. "Stop it, please."

She smiled coldly back at him. "Do you believe me now, when I say I'll take over this town?"

He nodded back. "Yes, fucking yes!" he whispered fiercely. "Just stop it before she kills him!"

The blonde girl had already picked up another chair and was getting ready to hit the unconscious Joey with it. Joey lay there defenseless on his back with his now deflated penis hanging out. The shop attendant seemed frozen, unable to intervene.

Jack stared out the shop window, then through the door. Where the hell was everyone? Cars were passing in the street, but there was no one on the sidewalk who could intervene. He was certain there were people entering and exiting the Domino's Pizza establishment next door, driving in and out, and getting in and out of cars, but none of them—not one of them it seemed—was even glancing towards the coffee shop. Was Cali mentally keeping people from coming this way while she gave him her 'demonstration?'

"Alright," Cali said. "I'll stop it. But don't you ever dare me again, or I'll do something really nasty."

Everything seemed to unfreeze in a way. Before the angry, weeping girl could smash the heavy chair over her boyfriend's head, Amos, the counter guy, crossed the shop and grabbed her. "Stop it! Stop it— you'll kill him."

Simultaneously it seemed like a haze cleared from her eyes too. She stared down at her boyfriend. "Oh my God—what the hell have I done!? Joey! Joey, wake up!"

She let the attendant take chair from her. Then she dropped down on her knees next to her boyfriend and began shaking him, all the while weeping.

To her relief Joey began reviving. He sputtered saliva and his eyes opened. "Kelly? What on earth just happened? Shit! My head." His eyes looked crossed, like he had a concussion. "Kelly what happened to you? Why are you all wet like this?"

The shop attendant helped Joey up to a chair. He looked as confused as the others. He'd seen what had happened. It had made no sense then, and it still made no sense now. "Hey, man, do you need me to call a doctor for you?"

"Why's my fly open?" Joey moaned.

"You don't remember?" the girl groaned.

"I don't remember a thing!"

Grinning, Cali got to her feet.

"Excuse me for a few minutes," she told Jack. "I got to take a little tinkle."

Jack nodded and she left him.

How in the world could she behave so cruelly just to make a point to me? he thought angrily. *These two kids didn't do a damn thing to her!*

He was so appalled by what he'd just witnessed—this horrible and ruthless display of her supernatural abilities—that he didn't dare look at her as she walked off towards the rear of the coffee shop, towards the door over which hung the restroom sign.

That was why Jack never saw Cali stroke the ass of the coffee shop attendant as she strode past him.

CHAPTER 17

Amos

Amos Green had no idea what was happening in his coffee bar. Well it wasn't actually his—he just worked here for his uncle—but the bar's ownership wasn't the point now.

However one viewed it, this had just become the craziest day of Amos's life.

First had been the guy who'd suddenly—completely out of the blue—begun masturbating, then come in his coffee cup and poured the mixture of coffee and come on his girlfriend. Then the girl herself, who'd decided to try and kill him. In Amos's twenty-five years of life he'd never seen a young woman that angry before. Yeah, sure, it must be complete shattering for someone to do what Joey had done to her, particularly if she had to go back to work, but still . . .

Amos was staring down at Joey. Joey who had blood all over his face now, and who, for the absolute life of him, looked clueless as to what had just happened.

Amos was wishing his uncle Mike were here to see things for himself—someone's salary was gonna have to replace that broken chair—when he felt the touch. Fingers gently brushing his buttocks.

Startled, he looked up. This hadn't been just some random, unavoidable contact such as might happen in a crowd. The fingers had lingered and gently pinched his ass.

He saw who'd done it. Or who must have done it. It was the raven-haired beauty who'd been sitting beside the window. She was past him now, heading for the restroom, while shaking her ass seductively. Oh, she had an ass alright, and she definitely could shake it.

Amos glanced nervously around, worried that her male friend had seen what she'd done. But no, the woman's companion was staring out of the window at the passing cars; not looking their way at all. Amos had no idea if the man—a new customer whose name he didn't yet know—was ignoring the action because he couldn't be bothered, or because he was disgusted with what he'd seen. On the other hand, Mr. Cooley, the old man who'd been reading the paper, couldn't stop staring at the troubled young couple. Mr. Cooley's old mouth hung half open, like he was under some kind of a spell; like he wanted to chide both 'kids,' but couldn't find the words; or like something was holding him back from doing so.

And that was the odd thing here. Amos too had felt like 'something' had held him back from interceding when the girl—Kelly—had picked up her chair and attacked her boyfriend with it. Actually his sense of a blockage extended further back, to when he'd first noticed Joey masturbating. At the time it was happening, he'd put his inability to react down to shock. But now, he wasn't sure. But if it hadn't been shock, what else could it possibly have been?

Amos looked back at the raven-haired woman. She'd slipped through the rear doorway now, leaving the strips of its bead curtain rattling against each other. He sighed. This was neither the time nor the place for flirting. And that was clearly all it was; there was no way that she really wanted him to come after her with her boyfriend here. Amos—tall and dark but skinny and with a large Adam's apple—held no illusions that he was Casanova.

And besides which, he had all this mess to clear up anyway: A metal chair in three or four pieces, a whole lot of liquid on the floor (and, aw shit, was that semen in that puddle by the girl's foot?), a shattered mug and two shattered plates.

"Look," he told Kelly as nicely as he could—he really did sympathize with her situation: if some guy had poured come on him, he'd have almost killed the man—"You guys are gonna have to pay for this damaged chair and tableware. Or my boss is gonna take it out of my salary. "

And that was the odd thing. Kelly too looked confused; Amos recalled the look in her eyes, when he'd grabbed her: like she'd been in a daze.

"I . . . I . . . d-do-don't know wha-wha-what came over me then," she sputtered. "Sure, we'll pay for the damages."

"How much did everything cost?" Joey managed to get out weakly. He'd wiped most of the blood from his face, but he had a nasty cut on his forehead which was going to need stiches. Thankfully, Joey had also packed his manhood away; Amos didn't need to be looking at the guy's penis. "Just add it to our bill," Joey said. "We're sorry for all the trouble."

"Yes, we are," his girlfriend agreed. "We'll pay for the damage right now."

"Yeah, sure," Amos said with a cautious smile. He was relieved that they weren't making a fuss about the breakage, but was growing even more perplexed by the minute. These two were clearly decent folk, so why on earth would they . . . *Almost like something suddenly came over them both.* "I'd better hurry it up then," he said. "That's a really bad cut you've got there, man. You need it looked at."

It was then that Amos felt the tugging on his mind. The pull was gentle at first, so that when he turned and walked away from Joey and Kelly, Amos really felt like he was heading to the service counter to get their receipt. But then, as he was about to turn in behind the counter, the pull became stronger, insistent, and instead of him reaching for the pad of receipt slips, he instead stepped through the bead curtain that led to the restroom.

Once through the door, the pull intensified yet further. Now it became an irresistible force in Amos's mind. He was vaguely aware of himself walking past the restroom door and instead opening the door to the storeroom at the end of the corridor.

He entered the storeroom and shut the door. She was in there, seated on a large box. She was already naked. On seeing her fantastic body in the nude, Amos's manhood instantly stiffened.

"I've been expecting you," she said, with a smile that both delighted and terrified Amos. "You're just the sort of man I like."

Amos didn't reply. His tongued felt glued to the roof of his mouth. His mouth in turn felt as dry as desert sand.

"Come here to me," she said, rising to her feet. "Undo your trousers and give me what I want."

Not bothering to watch him complying with her instruction, she turned and bent over the box, which she gripped to steady herself. She remained like that, with her buttocks pointed at him and her vagina ready and dripping.

Amos knew he had no choice but to make love to her. The force in his head that had summoned him in here still controlled him. He wasn't even aware that he'd entered her body until she began moaning. Then the unbelievable pleasure hit him and he began moaning too. She gripped the box; he gripped her hips; her iron control gripped his mind and moved his limbs.

They moved in sync like this, rocking back and forth, for several minutes. A portion of Amos's mind worried about the customers out front. Another portion of his mind assured him not to worry, that 'she' had them all 'under control.' A third portion of Amos's mind—that not under 'her' control—warned Amos of the danger he was in—that this she-devil of a woman was responsible for the earlier inexplicable happenings, and that he must break her control over him at whatever cost and flee for his life.

But it was too late. Even as this understanding of peril dawned on Amos, he began to feel himself draining away. He was still fucking her, his penis hard as bone inside the sweet cavern of her sex, but he felt himself 'going,' as it were; being sucked away into her. She was irresistible; he could already feel his orgasm rushing at him like a flood.

Amos was terrified. He was in greater pleasure than he'd ever thought sex could give one, and yet he knew this was his death. And he was utterly helpless to prevent it. He fought to reclaim control of his mind, yet was helpless against her iron domination of his psyche. She held him tight, squeezed him out like an orange; drank him like juice into herself.

She began to gasp loudly, her buttocks tensing against his thighs. "Yes, boy, I knew you'd be good for me. Oh, I'm almost here. Yes!"

She groaned loudly and stiffened in orgasm. "Oh, oh, OH!"

As she came, Amos came too, and as he came, he felt himself draining completely out of himself and into her.

NOOOOOO! his trapped psyche shrilled in terror as it drained away to become succubus food. *NOOOOOOOOOOOOOO!*

But there was no preventing the outcome. It was over.

He slipped out of her and crumpled to the floor.

CHAPTER 18

Cali

Cali considered the young man's remains. There was very little of him left now—just a withered husk on the floor, gray and emaciated and looking older than that really old man outside in the dining room.

But he'd been delicious. She licked her lips. This was the thing about living in the human world: out here the food was of so much higher quality. And one could get all of it at once. In the dream realm, the dream itself acted like a filter, protecting the sleeper from the succubus and restricting how much of his essence she could leech from him. One had to return again and again, and even then you never got enough to really tide you over.

She pulled her clothes on again, then returned to the dining room.

Jack was collapsed just inside the coffee shop entrance. While having sex, she'd sensed him trying to run away, so she'd drained him. He lay there gasping for breath, trying to claw his way out onto the sidewalk, but lacking even enough energy to think clearly. She was amused by Jack's confusion. She sensed his thoughts. He was wondering why no one at all was walking this way, no one who would notice and help him; and also why even those driving past didn't appear to notice his plight. She liked Jack, but he was a fool; he still had no idea of her incredible mind-control powers.

Jack was the only one in the coffee shop. The young couple had left. They were honest—they'd waited for the attendant to return, and when he'd delayed, they'd left two hundred dollars under a coffee cup to pay for the damage. The old man had likewise left; he'd insisted on escorting the couple to the hospital.

It was after they'd all gone that Jack had made his break for it.

Cali strode over to the doorway and squatted beside Jack. She smiled down at him. "I really enjoyed our lunch," she said in response to his pleading glances, then gently stroked his face to energize him again. "I'm full to bursting now. And now, I feel like relaxing a bit. So, let's drive home and go sit beside Maple Lake for a while."

She waited for him to get up from the floor, then they left together.

CHAPTER 19

Robin

Robin Thurgood was just about to get into her car when she spotted Jack Crannson down the street.

Her natural impulse was to call out to him. She curtailed it however. Not because he'd not hear her over the noise of the traffic—at the moment there were few cars on the road—but because he was with a woman. And this woman didn't look like a business associate of Jack's. Not with the way she was holding his arm and leaning on him. Not with the way she was dressed either, as if she was headed to a party somewhere . . . or to a seedy motel room. And certainly not with breasts that large, and swinging free at that. Even from here, Robin could tell that the other woman wasn't wearing a bra under her white tank top.

Jack too, wasn't dressed for work—having on just a short-sleeved shirt and jeans. Definitely not Monday-morning architect attire. But it was the woman's clothes Robin's enquiring mind fixed on:

Hey, are those Sam's clothes she's wearing? Yes, they are! That tank top and skirt are what she wore last time we went shopping, and the sandals too . . . ! Aw, Jack, what the hell are you up to?

So Robin didn't hail Jack, instead she watched him and his female companion closely. (She was standing ten yards from the couple, on the west side of the drive-in between the building that housed Domino's and the coffee shop and a dance studio. She was also on the farther side of her own brown car and thus concealed.)

The woman was very attractive. Robin—brunette, mid-thirties and rather 'mumsy' in appearance—felt instinctively jealous of her. As would Samantha too, she knew; even though Samantha was more attractive than herself. Robin felt jealous of Samantha too.

***

A month ago, Samantha Crannson had visited Robin. She'd been very upset.

"It's Jack," she'd complained. "He's moving out."

"You're separating?" Robin was unsure how the news made her feel. On the one hand, she felt a little thrill of delight—Samantha was so pretty and had a career and a rich husband and didn't seem to know how lucky she was that she wasn't married to a construction worker like Robin's husband Jerry. On the other hand, Robin felt for her as a friend. While not wealthy, her own marriage was a good and loving one, and she and Jerry had two children.

Childbearing was something Samantha and Jack seemed unable to find the time for. "Look, take a year or two off and have the kids," she'd urged Samantha. "You're a private investigator, meaning you work for yourself; and Jack's rich, so it ain't like you'll lack money while pregnant. Once the children come you can hire a nanny to look after them and resume work again."

But of course, Samantha had refused. "You don't understand," she'd said. "I just can't. I can't stop working."

And yes, Robin didn't understand. What was work for, except as a route to earn money to buy the things you needed? And if you already had money, what was the point of working more than you needed to? Robin herself wasn't a lazy woman, now that her children were in elementary school, she spent some of their school hours as a yoga instructor to supplement Jerry's income, but, the way she viewed it, if she who had possibly just a fifth of Samantha's money to get along on could be happy with her life, why couldn't her wealthy friend? Yes, Samantha always wore the nicest clothes, and drove a great car, and lived in a fantastic house—though it seemed she and her husband lived in their offices rather—but happiness was something she didn't have.

And see what her discontent had led to now?

"So you're separating?" Robin asked, still feeling that contradictory mix of sympathy and 'I told you so.'

"No, we're *not* separating," Samantha had corrected her. "He's just moving down here so as to be closer to work."

Robin had been unable to control herself. She'd leapt up and began angrily pacing her living room. "Work, work, work! What is it exactly that both of you are running away from?" she'd demanded. "Yourselves?"

"You just don't understand," Samantha had repeated as usual.

"No, I frigging don't," Robin had agreed. Then she'd softened her stance a little. Samantha had begun crying, dabbing her eyes dry with a tissue. Blonde hair, pale eyes perfect makeup—everything Robin wanted to be and have for herself—and yet she looked like a mess.

"Stop crying," Robin said, going to sit beside her.

"I can't help it," Samantha sobbed. "You're right, Robin—I do think we're running away from ourselves. I think Jack's moving down here to Bridgeport to get away from me." She'd wept some more. I love Jack, Robin. I really do. It's just that . . . I don't know why I feel I have to put work first in everything I do."

"Well . . . work's not bad . . . but the way you guys handle your business . . . you never let your hair down and enjoy your money." She'd gestured around her own modest living room. "Jerry and I, we make do. We relax and laugh together. Sure, sometimes we fight. But he puts me first, and though sometimes I'd prefer to have more money to spend or this year's model of car, I can appreciate that, you know?" Then seeing Samantha looking about to start crying again, Robin had looked for a way to comfort her.

"Hey, tell you what I'll do," she said finally. "How about if I keep an eye on Jack for you?"

Robin had dabbed the fresh tears from her eyes and stared at Robin. "Huh? What do you mean?"

She'd shrugged. "Not what you think. You're the private investigator, not me. What I'm thinking is, seeing as he's here in town now—I can find some excuse to drop in on him now and then and see if there's any signs of another woman living with him." She'd stared cannily at Samantha. "That's what you're really worried about, isn't it? That he's not just moving out because you're pushing him away, but that he's found someone else?"

Samantha nodded. "I have thought of that. I didn't really believe it, but . . ."

"Okay, it's settled then. I'll call him up once he moves down here and check the place out. Even if he's alone in the house, he won't be able to hide all the signs of another house occupant. One place I'll look is the kitchen, see what's stocked in the fridge. How much shopping does Jack do usually?"

Samantha shook her head. "Almost none. I'm the one who buys everything. Whenever I'm not home, he mostly eats out."

"So if I arrive there and find the fridge well-stocked, we'll know he's seeing someone and you can either file for divorce or raise such a fuss that he'll ditch his mistress."

"I don't really believe Jack has a mistress," Samantha said. Then she looked helpless. "But I'm travelling so much out of the state that anything can happen while I'm gone. And him living alone in such a large house."

"So, I'll confirm that for you then," Robin said brightly, "and then you'll have nothing to worry about."

***

Staring now across the turnoff as Jack and the black-haired woman readied to enter his SUV, Robin Thurgood couldn't help but feel intensely disappointed in him. So *this* was why he'd refused to let her come visit him at home? He'd claimed he was tired, but she'd not bought that excuse at all. And she saw that she'd been right.

Well at least now I know what's been tiring him out, she thought grimly, ironically unaware of just how correct her deduction was.

She realized she didn't have much time. Samantha, being a private eye, would prefer concrete evidence of her man's infidelity. Robin intended to present her with such evidence.

She'd already gotten out her cellphone; now she tapped on the camera app, switched it from photo to video and ducking slightly behind her car, began recording the happenings outside the coffee shop.

She was in luck. Jack and the woman were having an argument of some kind by the hood of the SUV. Maybe it was merely a discussion, but Jack looked displeased about something.

Maybe she wants another Gucci handbag and he's not willing to fork over the cash. A bitch like this has 'mistress' written all over her. She doesn't look like she's worked a day in her life. And Sam's been slaving away at Jack's side all these years . . . well not exactly at his side, they've each been going their separate ways since their marriage, but that's not the frigging point here! The point is that Sam deserves better treatment than she's getting from Jack!

Her righteous indignation at fever pitch, Robin recorded about five minutes of video. That was more than enough. She got the woman on tape, rubbing her breasts against Jack, pointing an angry finger at him, then smiling and kissing him on the lips, before walking around seductively towards the front passenger seat.

Jack had unlocked the car doors with his key fob, and the woman just had to get into the vehicle and sit down, but she didn't. She pulled the door open, then with her hand still on the door handle, she froze.

Robin had the sudden impression that the black-haired woman had realized someone was watching her. Something about the way she'd stopped, like an animal sensing danger.

Jack was already inside the SUV, staring ahead like he was on drugs. That was odd too, how Jack was behaving—Robin had noted that he looked tired, but she couldn't bother herself over how much sex he'd been having.

And Robin also had other concerns now. The woman looked up and stared across the SUV's windshield, directly at her.

"Oh, shit—she's seen me!" Robin gasped, wanting to duck into cover, but unable to.

Their eyes locked across the road. At that moment a truck turned off the road and passed between them, momentarily separating their gazes. But when it was gone, Robin and the woman were still standing in exactly the same positions as previously, and still staring at each other.

Staring at the woman opposite, Robin suddenly felt terrified. She felt as if her head was expanding. And, though this was clearly impossible, she also felt like she heard the woman's voice in her head . . . "You're useless to me as food," the voice seemed to say, "but don't you dare meddle in my affairs, or you'll discover just how ruthless I am."

The moment passed and there were no more words in Robin's head. The woman outside the Almost Heaven Coffees shop was no longer looking her way. She got into the vehicle beside Jack. He reversed out of the parking lot and they drove off.

Robin, however, didn't feel fine anymore. Watching the silver SUV depart, she felt cold; really, really cold. She was trembling from head to foot, and was more scared than she'd been in a long time. Once Jack had turned the corner, she got into her own car and drove off in the opposite direction, shivering with fear all the while.

CHAPTER 20

Jack

When Jack and Cali arrived back home that Monday afternoon, first they spent half and hour sitting and walking by the lake.

Watching the succubus walk barefoot beside the water, Jack was once more struck by the contradictions she presented. Now, she once again seemed like a normal human woman, standing and laughing in the water, slipping and almost falling into it when a startled fish startled her in turn, giggling and pulling him in alongside her as if they were lovers. Just like during their drive through town, Cali's delight was so ingenuous and unfeigned that Jack almost felt things were normal between them.

But of course things weren't normal. And this fact was soon rammed home to him again.

***

Once they were back inside the house, Cali's playful demeanor altered. She immediately took Jack upstairs to the north bedroom.

She led him across the glowing ring on the floor and pushed him down on the bed. "Like I said, you'll be living in here from now on."

Then she fucked Jack extra-hard, leaving him so drained afterwards that he was no threat to her. He lay there in her succubus bed, half-alive, but seemingly even closer to death, floating in and out of consciousness. He was unsure if he was awake or dreaming.

"Perfect," Cali said, grinning down at him, while licking from her lips the semen from the last blowjob which had literally blown his mind. "Just be a good boy and remain in here. I drop by to see you now and again."

Then Cali left the bedroom, locking Jack inside it.

CHAPTER 21

Casper

"What the hell?" Caspar asked Laney that evening at home.

She nodded. She was on the living room couch. Her eyes were red; she'd been crying profusely all evening. Her hands clasped a Coke can. Dray was on the floor by the TV, but this time the TV was turned off. Even with what (from the evidence of empty cans littering the living room floor) seemed to be his fifth beer of the evening in his hand, Dray didn't look much better than Laney

"Yeah, baby," Laney said. "It happened a little bit after you left on that third delivery. Dray had a delivery to make too, but then we heard a commotion next door in the coffee shop, so we went over there. The shop was full of confused people and Mr. Green was calling for an ambulance. He looked sick like he needed an ambulance himself. Dray and I kept asking folks what the matter was, only no one really seemed to know; though there was some blood on the floor and one of the chairs was broken." She paused and sucked on her Coke. "So at first we just assumed there'd been a fight in there, and someone had gotten wounded. Then Dray asked for Amos, and that was when Mr. Green turned and pointed to the back room area—you know, where the toilets are? 'In the storeroom,' was all he gasped, looking like he'd collapse right there from shock. Like everyone else, we assumed maybe *he* needed medical attention and he meant he'd sent Amos into the storeroom to fetch something for him, like a mop to clean up the mess on the floor. So we went in there to look for him. And . . ." Her voice broke. "And that's where we found Amos." She looked at her brother, her eyes pleading with him to continue the story.

"Shit, bro," Dray said after a swig of beer. "I ain't never seen the likes of it. I mean, it didn't even look like Amos no more. Just some old withered up prune of a man who seemed more aged than Mr. Bannering."

"What?" Caspar yelped in disbelief.

"It's true," Laney said, having recovered a little. "We only knew it was Amos because of his clothes—you remember those black Nikes of his? And his hair, you know that funny haircut he had. It was utterly insane. He was lying there on the floor, dead and withered down to nothing—"

"His skin was flaking off," Dray interjected. "That's how fucking dry he was."

"—And, Cass, the craziest thing of all? You know what that was?"

Caspar shook his head. "No idea, baby. Just tell me."

She gulped and wiped fresh tears from her cheeks. "His pants were down around his ankles . . . like he'd . . . like he'd been having sex. Or was about to have a pee in there. But couldn't have been peeing because the toilets were next door."

Dray gulped more beer and shook his head. If he'd looked bothered before, now he *really* looked bothered. "That's why it was so insane to view: Amos's dick was the only part of him that didn't look shriveled. The rest? Just imagine one of those movies where grave robbers unearth some guy after he's been buried for years. You know how those corpses look? Like everything inside's been sucked out of them and you're just viewing skin stretched over bones? Well, that was what Amos looked like."

Caspar looked at Laney for confirmation. She nodded.

"Then the paramedics arrived and got us both out of there," Dray finished. "We could see that they too were confused as fuck though."

Caspar sat beside Laney on the couch and held her tight. Amos Green dead? And under such weird conditions? What the hell?

CHAPTER 22

Robin

"I don't believe it," Robin Thurgood said, joining her husband in the living room. "I just don't believe it. Jerry, what the hell do you make of this?"

Robin had just gotten back from putting her two children to bed. Her husband Jerry, a stocky man with prematurely gray hair, stopped channel surfing on the TV and accepted the cellphone she offered him, then watched the video she was playing. Robin stood beside him, waiting for his comments.

After about a minute of watching the video, Jerry paused it and stared at her in incredulity.

"What the hell's he doing?" The video showed Jack Crannson apparently holding a conversation with himself by the hood of his car. Gesturing at the air. At a point the conversation degenerated into a vicious argument which might have made sense if there was someone else there with him. But Jack was the only one caught on camera.

"He wasn't alone," Robin protested. "There was a woman with him; that's why I recorded him in the first place."

Jerry Thurgood scowled. "Hon, I already told ya to leave the Crannson's alone. If Jack and Sam wanna work themselves to death, let them work themselves to death. It's no damn business of yours or mine."

"Robin thinks he's cheating on her."

"Shit. You women, and your goddamned jealousies. Robbie, the guy's a goddamned workaholic. Where's he gonna find the time to cheat on her?" He gestured at the phone. "What did you plan on telling Sam anyway—that her husband's dating the goddamned air?"

Robin shook her head angrily. She wasn't angry at Jerry, but at the confusion. She was very confused.

"But I did see that woman," she protested helplessly. "Jerry, there *was* a woman with Jack. I saw her, they were both outside the Domino's Pizza shop. She was tall, was beautiful and had black hair!"

"I'm not arguing with ya on that. You just didn't film her. Or if you did, where the hell is she?"

Robin sat beside him on the couch. She looked defeated. "Honey, that's what *I'd* like to know now."

Jerry didn't say anything else for a while. He replayed the video, watching it with troubled eyes.

"Well, one of you'se crazy, that's for sure," Jerry said finally.

"One of us?" Robin gaped at him. "You think I'm crazy too?"

Jerry shook his head. "Just hear me out. Of course, I don't think you're crazy, hon, but that's sure as hell how it looks, ain't it? See, either you're nuts for claiming there was a woman with Jack Crannson when you filmed this; or he's nutty for behaving like he's talking to someone else." He grinned at her. "Baby, take your pick. Who's nuts—you or him?"

Robin felt trapped. There was no way she could explain what she'd seen, and without video evidence, no way to prove her allegations to Samantha either.

Jerry wasn't done speaking though. "But still, I think you gotta alert Sam to this." He played the video for a short while longer, then nodded to himself. "Yeah, I got a real bad feeling 'bout this one: If Sam don't come back home right now from wherever she's run off to—" He looked questioningly at Robin.

"Indiana," she filled in for him. "She's travelling around, tracking down a runaway teen."

"Well, if she doesn't get back soonest from there, when she does arrive in town she'll most likely be going to visit Jack in the loony bin." He handed Robin's phone back to her. "Any luck with calling her so far?"

"No, it's still switched off. But I left her a voicemail message. She leaves her phone off because it might distract her in a tight spot. She says she almost got killed once, when Jack called her during a gunfight."

Jerry looked curious. "Gunfight?"

Robin nodded. "According to Sam, she and two hoodlums had been shooting at each other for a while. She was trapped inside a warehouse, hiding from them, and they had no idea where she was, but she could hear them. She'd just heard them saying they were certain she'd escaped and that they'd better leave before the police arrived because of the gunshot noises, when her phone buzzed. She'd left it on silent and vibrate. Unfortunately, she was pressed against an empty metal drum at the time and the drum amplified the vibrations. The hoodlums turned and immediately began firing at her again. Sam was fortunate that the cops arrived right then and arrested all three of them, herself included." Robin nodded. "So since then, the phone stays in her motel room most times."

Jerry nodded. "Makes kinda sense that, except, according to you, sometimes she don't answer the phone for days, and . . . if she won't pick up, how the hell are you gonna tell her that her husband's cracking up under the pressure of overwork?"

Robin didn't reply. "Turn on the TV sound," she told Jerry, to change the topic. "The new *Walking Dead* episode is coming on."

While Jerry fiddled with the remote, Robin tried to make sense of what had happened to her video recording. *Did I really film nothing? But no, I definitely didn't! I saw that woman, for real. That slut! And she . . . she . . .*

The woman's warning floated through her mind: *You're useless to me as food . . . don't you dare meddle in my affairs . . . I'm ruthless.*

Then Robin smiled. Maybe Jerry was right and she'd seen nothing. Because the shrinks all said that once you began hearing voices in your head, then you were definitely crazy for real. *I like Jerry's analysis: Jack's the crazy one here; not me. I'd better get word across to Sam about her home-front crisis. Once she sees this video she'll understand how serious matters are.*

Before relaxing to enjoy her favorite television zombie drama, Robin took the time to send Samantha a detailed message on her iPhone explaining the situation, and also attached the video she'd recorded. She left out mention of the black-haired woman, wrote instead that Jack was acting erratically and might soon be publicly embarrassed.

She was now able to relax, accepting that she'd fulfilled her obligations to a friend to the best of her ability. If that video didn't alert Samantha that she needed to get her ass home, pronto, nothing would.

CHAPTER 23

Dray

Wednesday. At about one-thirty in the afternoon

Utterly disgusted with himself, Drayfuss Springer sat in the Domino's Pizza staff room, staring at the ceiling and pondering his lack of a satisfactory sex life.

Shit, man, how long am I gonna remain a virgin for?

More than once, Laney had told Dray that being a male virgin at age twenty ought to be made a criminal offence. Dray was inclined to agree with her. There were girls of all shapes and sizes everywhere; why couldn't *he* find one to date? Outside of porn, Dray had never seen a woman naked.

Dray was tired of his timidity where girls were concerned.

Take just now, for instance. He was on the second shift today, but arriving to work early, he'd stopped by the Almost Heaven Coffees shop next door to find out the latest news on Amos Green's weird death. There were no customers in the shop, all the chairs upturned on the tables and the 'Closed' sign had been on the door.

Still Dray, knowing Amos's uncle Mr. Green, had pushed his way in, and who had he met there in the coffee shop if not Betsy York? Betsy had been mopping up when Dray walked in. She'd smiled at Dray and told him she'd just been employed by Mr. Green, and that they'd be reopening tomorrow, but dammit, wasn't that just such a horrible thing that had happened to Amos?

Dray had agreed, mostly nodding. Once again he'd found himself tongue-tied where an attractive member of the opposite sex was concerned.

And Betsy was hot. She was shapely, with short brown hair and sweet lips. Dray just imagined himself kissing those lips of hers, then her wrapping them around his hard cock and sucking him into a state of ecstasy while he simultaneously lapped at her juicy pussy. But there

88

the beautiful erotic fantasy ended; ended because Dray knew he'd never work up the nerve to ask Betsy out on a date. And if you couldn't even date a girl, how the hell were you ever going to wind up in bed with her?

It shouldn't have been hard to ask her out. He and Betsy had attended high school together at Bridgeport. They'd been friends even back then.

But—Dray cursed his timidity—all he'd done this afternoon was stand there like all he wanted to do was catch up on old times with her and explain how he worked at the Domino's next door, while for her part, Betsy leaned on her mop and smiled sweetly and asked how his sister Laney was and her boyfriend Cass too, and how his older sister and her family were doing over in Japan? Then they'd parted, with Dray promising to drop in for a coffee occasionally.

He'd left the coffee shop fuming at himself. He felt utterly livid and stupid. During their conversation, Betsy had suggested that she was single. Dray had wanted to ask her out, but . . . but . . .

So now he sat there staring at the wall and wondering what to do. One thing was for sure; pretty Betsy York right next door presented an opportunity for him to lose his virginity. Or if not that, at least for him to go out on a few dates and get over his timidity.

Resolving to ask Caspar's advice to get him started, Dray got up and went to begin his shift.

***

Halfway through the afternoon, a pizza order came in for someone on Maple Lake Road.

Joe, the cook who'd boxed the pizza, was about to give the delivery to another carrier, but Dray stopped him. "I'll take it," he said. "Maple Lake's where I live. The client's address is right on my street."

Joe handed the pizza over. "Alright, man, here you go."

Dray rode his bike off towards Maple Lake.

***

The pizza delivery was for Mrs. Armstead, an old woman whose grandchildren were spending the summer with her. She paid Dray; he thanked her and left. He was about to wheel his motorbike right and head back to town, when he changed his mind and turned the bike left instead.

The Armstead house was at the top of the east side of the Maple Lake Road loop. Dray's house was in the middle of that same east side road. He'd just decided to touch base at home before returning to work.

Dray had just had a brainwave. Caspar should be home at the moment. Dray figured he'd stop by the house and ask Caspar how to go about asking Betsy York out. He wasn't certain Laney would be home too, but if she was he'd ask her advice also. She'd likely mock him first, but Dray could live with that. He felt he was in desperate straits.

Come hell or lake water, he thought grimly, looking across Maple Lake as he thought this, *I'm gonna ask Betsy York out today. I need to get laid this month, or I'm gonna be a virgin all my life. If I don't lose my virginity this month, I'd better just go into the priesthood.*

At last Dray had a plan.

***

Like Caspar had done the other night, Dray slowed down as he approached Mr. Crannson's house. He too had just noticed his neighbor's beautiful houseguest standing at the foot of the driveway.

Too bad she's got her clothes on, Dray thought dreamily as he approached her. *A body like that . . .*

Shimmering body of water reflecting the mid-afternoon sun on his left, he coasted the motorbike toward her, wondering if he dared stop and say hello. This wouldn't be asking for a date. He'd just introduce himself as her next door neighbor, ask if she needed any help with anything . . . and yes, get an eyeful of her tits. Too bad it had to be just an eyeful, though. Dray could have done with a mouthful of the lady's breasts. Even under the tee shirt she currently had on, her breasts seemed so perfect as to defy belief.

Dray got closer still to her. She'd initially been staring at something across the road, but then, as if she sensed him watching her, she suddenly turned and looked right at him.

And next thing, she did the one thing that Dray would never ever, ever expect a woman that gorgeous to do:

She pulled up the hem of her tee shirt and flashed her breasts at him. She held the tee shirt up over her head, so Dray got a real eyeful. He'd been wrong about how great her breasts were. Dray had never seen breasts as perfect as these, not even in porn.

The magnificent mammaries had an unprecedented effect. Dray lost control of the steering of the bike, and rode it up over the curb and onto the sidewalk. The engine seemed to stall then, and the bike rolled freely towards the woman, who was just lowering her tee shirt again.

Time seemed to slow down. Dray had seemingly lost all control of his motorbike. He couldn't get it to turn either left or right and the brakes refused to work too.

Horrified, he waved and yelled at the woman to get out of the way. She didn't move at all. She didn't appear perturbed in the least that he was about to ram into her. Dray valiantly fought the handlebars to get them to alter direction, but they seemed locked. He lifted his hands to shield his face from the impact.

But then, right before the moment when he was sure to have hit her, the front wheel twisted hard to the left and Dray found himself riding through Mr. Crannson's rose hedge instead. Speeding across the well-kept lawn towards the white two-story house.

Behind him, he could hear the woman laughing. Oh, but she had a lovely laugh, tinkling like bells. He was still thinking this when his bike came to an abrupt halt against a stone and he went flying through the air.

He landed hard and wound up stunned.

CHAPTER 24

Dray & Cali

It took Dray awhile to get himself mentally organized again. The primary reason for this was . . . well, Dray couldn't shake the conviction that his *not* hitting the woman hadn't been an accident: he'd felt something—a paranormal force or whatever—wrench the handlebars from his control and redirect the motorbike.

But that was ludicrous, right?

At least I'm alive and I don't seem to have broken anything. Dray was actually relieved. He'd realized he'd been fortunate as to which direction he'd ridden off the sidewalk. He could just as easily have skidded right instead of left and wound up half drowning himself in the lake.

"Hey, are you okay?"

He rolled over onto his back and looked up. Like a vision, the most beautiful woman he'd ever seen—yes, it was her, gorgeous and with incredible nipples pricking the front of her tee shirt—staring down at him.

He was speechless.

She seemed to realize that he wouldn't say anything. "I'm really sorry for teasing you like that," she said gently. "But seriously . . . are you alright? Here, let me help you up."

Dray gave her his hand and next thing he knew he was up on his feet. He looked around. The blue Domino's motorbike lay on its side. The front wheel had come off and the pizza storage case too had rolled off toward the trees.

Dray shook his head at the sight. "Thank heavens that's not my neck," he said. Then he looked at the woman more cautiously. "Why in the world would you do a thing like that to a guy?"

She stuck out her hand. "Let's get better acquainted first. My name's Cali. I'm a friend of Jack's."

Dray assumed 'Jack' meant Mr. Crannson. He shook her hand. "I'm Dray Springer. Your next door neighbor. But, Cali, please for fuck's sake, don't ever do that again to anyone. These breasts of yours can kill a guy. I ain't joking."

She laughed her pretty laugh. "Come inside and have a drink with me."

"My bike. It's ruined."

"It'll still be ruined afterwards. You might as well come in the house. If the bike's repairable, I'll split the costs with you."

"That's nice of you."

She laughed again. "Not really. It *is* largely my fault that you had your accident." She shook her breasts at him for emphasis, then turned and walked off towards the house, calling over her shoulder: "Come."

Dray, who to his surprise had just realized he was having no difficulty whatsoever chatting with Cali, followed after her.

***

There was a young man in a business suit seated in the living room.

"Hi," Dray said.

The young man didn't reply. He just sat there. He was staring at the TV, but the TV was off.

"Don't mind him," Cali replied to Dray's bemused glance at her. "He's an architect—one of Jack's staff. At the moment he's busy picturing a building in his head or something like that." She grimaced mockingly. "Says it takes intense concentration."

Dray nodded. Personally he found it creepy the way the guy was sitting there with his eyes blank. He was glad to leave the young man behind in the living room.

Cali led Dray through the house and into the kitchen. There, she merely got out a bottle of white wine from the drinks cabinet and then walked out again, leading him next along a short hallway to a downstairs bedroom at the north side of the house.

By now Dray had an erection. The body moving in front of his was so seductive he couldn't help it. All he could think of doing was grabbing hold of Cali and sticking his manhood deep into her womanhood. He didn't understand where all his previous shyness had vanished too. Now he felt bold, ready to take on a thousand women in bed—so long as they were all this one woman.

And yes, Dray did feel a little odd, as if a supernatural force—maybe even the same one that had crashed his motorcycle—had taken control of his mind, but the control seemed natural. After all, wasn't losing his virginity what he wanted more than anything else in this world? Hadn't he prayed to Heaven that this woman, this one who even now was shutting the guest bedroom door behind them and pulling off her clothes, was the one he wanted to lose his virginity to? And Heaven had answered his prayers and he had her now and he was going to fuck her really hard and have his first sexual experience that didn't involve his hands with her.

"Yes, you are, Dray," she said as if plucking the thoughts from his mind. "You're gonna fuck me so hard that I'll shit come. That's what you want, baby, isn't it? To become a man? A real woman-fucking man?"

She turned to him, naked and more perfect than he'd ever imagined a woman could be. She was complete seduction, and though now her eyes looked evil and hungry, he knew that giving himself to her—feeding himself to her—was all he wanted.

She sat on the edge of the bed and poured herself a drink. "Well, what are you waiting for, Dray? Take your damn clothes off and join me."

Dray got undressed in record time. Then, despite his overwhelming haste to penetrate her, he accepted a drink from her.

They finished the drinks and she pushed him down flat on the bed. "Let's go slow," she said mockingly, all the niceness suddenly gone from her face and voice. "You'll live longer that way."

"I can't wait any longer," Dray pleaded. "I feel like I'm gonna die if I don't have you right away."

"You'll die anyway," Cali said unsympathetically. "I'm just keeping you alive a few minutes longer."

"I don't care!" Dray yelled and grabbed her, rolling their bodies around so that she was under him now. "I have to come inside you. This is the first time for me. Stop being a prickteaser and wasting my damn time!"

She laughed loudly and spread her legs wide. "You're the kind of man I really like . . . the impatient kind." She grabbed his hard manhood and steered it inside her pussy.

Dray gasped on entering her. Yes, he'd known sex was fantastic, but never that it was this fantastic. Oh, shit, oh shit, oh shit! Dazzling sensations coursed through him over and over again.

Cali moved her hips up to meet him; she wrapped him in her arms; locked him in her legs. She lifted her mouth up to his and sucked on his tongue. She actually felt sorry for him. It was truly sad that a person's first sexual experience would prove to be their last.

Dray thrust and thrust into her, reaching such joyous extremes of pleasure that later, when everything reversed and Cali began leeching him into herself, he had no idea that he was being emptied.

The room turned red around him and it seemed as if he was upstairs, not downstairs anymore, and both of them were fucking on an old musty bed, and there was a burning red ring on the floor and a dried-up man beside them on the bed . . .

And then suddenly Dray wanted to scream in horror as he drained away but it was much too late. Much much too late then.

But at least he'd lost his virginity first.

CHAPTER 25

The History of the Bed

At the same time that Drayfuss Springer was shriveling away downstairs, Jack Crannson was writhing in agony upstairs. Not a physical agony (he was too weak to feel pain), but a spiritual torment.

The bed. The bed.

The bed was a prison, the red ring its walls. Now that he was weakened, the bed gripped him like a magnet; keeping him for itself.

Cali had been right: this wasn't the place to be. Jack felt no hunger or thirst, for the bed nourished him. It fed him with just enough energy to ensure that he wouldn't leave it, either by dying or by getting up and walking away from it.

So Jack lay there, his mind slowly filling with images. The images seeped up from the old mattress into his head, forming a tapestry of history. Jack saw things that had happened in the far past and gained a proper understanding of the present.

In a way, it was the story of the bed; in another way, it was Cali's story:

***

On a stormy windswept evening in Bridgeport back in 1978, five teenagers sat around an Ouija board.

It happened in this very house, up in this same bedroom.

Back then, this was 15-year-old Tracy Bannering's bedroom, and kids being what they are, she and four of her closest friends had decided to hold a séance for the fun of it. The Ouija board they used belonged to Tracy's best friend Katie Taylor, who had to sneak it into the house because, while not exactly religious, Tracy's father William was very wary of objects that seemed to be doing 'the Devil's work.'

William Bannering was right to be wary. (In Jack's vision, Mr. Bannering was a vibrant man in his late thirties, with a full head of dark hair, a rather large nose and dark eyes.) But that fateful evening, at the same time as his daughter and her friends were attempting to summon the spirits of the dead, William and his wife Mildred were down in a restaurant in the south part of Bridgeport having dinner with friends.

For the five teens in attendance, the séance was an overwhelming success. Their first contact had been with the spirit of 5-year-old Tommy Barrick, the younger brother of Sue Barrick, one of those in attendance. Tommy had died a fortnight ago after being hit by a car. Now, speaking primarily through Tracy, who was surprised to discover she had some powers as a medium, Tommy assured them all that he was in a lovely white place with lots of angels everywhere. Sue wept and felt some closure after her brother's death.

Emboldened by their success, the teens tried again, this time casting in the ether sea for Melissa Parks, who'd been in their high school class but had gotten murdered one night last winter. At first they'd run into a roadblock: Melissa either wouldn't or couldn't talk to her. But then, the Ouija board's planchette began sliding under their fingers again. "Melissa's not available at the moment," another presence had replied, "but I'll talk to you. I'm a close friend of hers. My name is Cali. I'm a succubus."

The teens realized they'd latched on to a non-human spirit. And a sexy one at that. Barry and Marty, the two boys present, had whooped with delight. Once Tracy gave her approval, Cali had possessed her. Cali/Tracy sat there with her eyes rolled back so only the whites showed, and answered all the teen's questions about sex in the afterlife. Yes, there was a Hell, she assured them, but it was great fun to be there—you had sex all the time with no worries about disease and pregnancies. And so on . . .

Then Cali urged them to experiment sexually with each other.

Sue Barrick and Katie Taylor immediately began a lesbian scene. The pair had been wanting to fuck each other for close to a year; this séance provided the perfect opportunity.

The two boys watched them go down on each other for a few minutes, then:

"Come and make love to me," Cali/Tracy had demanded. Barry and Marty hurried over and stripped Tracy naked. She was a hot girl and they'd gotten right down to making love to her. Tracy had been a virgin too. Barry had been the one who'd deflowered her—which was exactly what Cali had wanted to happen. Once the girl was 'blooded' she could possess her for good. For the moment, though, the orgy continued. The boys and girls all slept with each other; with Barry and Marty even doing a double-penetration on Sue, who came so hard during the action that she fainted.

After that everyone cleaned themselves up. They were all dressed and well-behaved again by the time Tracy's parents got back home.

The teens were all exhilarated at what had happened, and yet rather perplexed that the sex had gotten so out of hand. Still, there were suggestions of their holding another séance soon.

Fast forward two weeks, and Tracy Bannering began behaving strangely. Cali, now firmly resident in the girl, saw no reason for her to go to school, so Tracy began cutting classes. Also, because Cali was a sex demon, young Tracy's sex drive went through the roof. Not only did she begin masturbating all the time, but she also (on those rare days when she attended classes) began soliciting the boys at school for sex. And the teachers. And men she didn't know from Adam on the streets. She dressed in the most revealing outfits she could wear without getting arrested and hung on street corners soliciting men for sex.

1978 Bridgeport was an easygoing place, but soon enough Tracy got a reputation as the town slut. Her parents didn't know what to do. William and Mildred Bannering had no idea why their quiet, well-behaved, and A-grade studious daughter who'd wanted to go to university to become a neurosurgeon had suddenly degenerated to a hooker. More than once had the town cops brought the girl home after finding her on some street corner, with or without male companionship. The men were generally given a beating and run off; William Bannering was friends with the Bridgeport chief of police and no one wanted the scandal of a trial. And besides, in every single case, Tracy was the one who'd accosted the men; never the other way around. In fact, the police chief told William: "Will, if the girl carries on like this, you might wind up having to commit her for her own good."

Cali, of course, was delighted. She was finally having all the sex she'd ever wanted—feeding as much as she liked. The sex didn't really drain Tracy's male partners, and the teen herself enjoyed the endless orgasms she was having.

But the succubus was either unaware or just didn't care that she was going too far.

Something had to be done. Almost at his wits end by then, William Bannering began enquiring around his daughter's friends, asking if they knew why she'd suddenly gone off the rails. Had she been sexually assaulted by someone?

Finally Sue Barrick told him about the séance they'd held in his house that distant night (this was three months later) and about the spirit they'd summoned.

William was stunned. The supernatural? But still, at least now he had clear knowledge of what the problem was. All he needed to do was find the solution.

***

The first set of images faded. Jack seemed to become the bed, its memories filled his head. More images floated and gelled and strung themselves out in a logical sequence. The tale resumed:

***

It was night. Once again people were in this same north bedroom. This time however, the ritual wasn't a summoning, but rather an exorcism.

Tracy lay on her bed, clothed in a long white nightgown. She was drugged, unable to flee. Dressed in black, her parents stood on either side of the bed. Mildred Bannering's was face as white as if she was mourning. William, though his expression was more stoic, didn't actually look much better than his wife did. He was worried that this wouldn't succeed; had no idea what to do if it didn't.

The exorcist was a middle-aged man in a red suit. Mr. Sykes. He had short blonde hair, a long beard, and piercing blue eyes. Mr. Sykes's face was painted bone white. He looked more demon than human.

The room was dotted about with lit red candles; their flames dancing left and right.

Mr. Sykes began intoning a prayer . . . or was it a spell? (Jack—sharing the bed's memories—didn't know for certain.) The words were guttural and frightening, and the fear the exorcist's strange speech produced in William and Mildred Bannering was clear on the couple's faces.

And then Tracy began jerking on the bed. She flung her limbs back and forth and seemed to be screaming silently. And finally, a black jelly spilled from her mouth and dissolved into the air over her face. Tracy immediately fell back limp and lay motionless and sweating.

"She is free now," the exorcist said simply, his white-painted face impassive. "The demoness Cali has left her."

His words were true. The ritual was a success. The next morning, exactly as if they're been no intervening interlude, Tracy got up, dressed up decently, picked up her schoolbooks and headed for class. Everyone was astonished. A smart girl, she quickly caught up on the classes she'd missed. At home, realizing how far back she'd fallen in her schoolwork, Tracy would spend entire nights poring over her textbooks, working hard to get her neurosurgeon dreams back on track. Sometimes, in the morning her mother would find her asleep at her study desk, her head on her books.

It didn't last though. A month later, Cali made her reentry into Tracy. The next morning, Tracy dressed up like a slut again and was finally found sucking off a trucker at the Jane Lew Truck Stop. The cops broke the trucker's left arm for him and took the teenager back home.

William Bannering sent for the exorcist again.

"Where is she now?" Mr. Sykes asked.

"No idea," William said flatly. "She comes home about once a week. And now, she looks like she's doing hard drugs too." Then he looked really bothered. "Look, man, Tracy will be eighteen in two weeks time."

Mr. Sykes laughed. "Yes, I understand: You need to get this over with before she turns eighteen and, no longer a minor, can more or less do what she likes; including completely ruin her life by going to jail for soliciting."

William nodded.

Mr. Sykes laughed coldly again. "Don't worry. I know exactly what to do. But it will cost you, William."

William Bannering shrugged. "How much? Get that demon out of Tracy for good and you can have everything in my bank account."

Mr. Sykes shook his head. "Not money, William. It will cost you both blood and *diligence*. All your life, you'll need to be on your guard against a recurrence."

Will nodded. "Fine."

"Good. I'll explain the details later, once the evil spirit has departed again. For now, it is good that your daughter is currently away from home. We've a few preparations to make before her return."

**

The images sped through Jack's head again—furniture being moved out of Tracy's room, bars being fixed on the windows, and finally . . . the bed being trucked in from out of town.

The bed wasn't the type one bought in Ashley's Furniture store next to Walmart. It appeared custom made. It was built of thick wood and there were a number of cryptic symbols carved on the bedposts.

Then, Jack saw Cali/Tracy, drunk and unsuspecting anything was amiss, walking up to the front door and ringing . . . then banging impatiently . . . Tracy being let in . . . Tracy being knocked out by her father with a sharp blow to the head, tied up and carried upstairs . . . a phone call to Mr. Sykes . . . the exorcist arriving at the house in his trademark red suit, with his face already painted white (Jack wondered how he'd pulled that stunt without the cops hassling him) . . . William and Mildred and Mr. Sykes climbing the stairs to the north bedroom and locking the door behind them . . .

**

The new bed sat in the exact center of the north bedroom. Tracy lay on it, stripped naked. Once the door was locked, Mr. Sykes had told her father to untie her and her mother to undress her. As if the room had tranquilized her, Tracy wasn't moving. She lay there staring at the ceiling and looking very angry.

"And now we'll begin," the black exorcist told William.

Mr. Sykes now bent beside his attaché case—it actually looked to Jack like a doctor's bag—and brought out several items. One of these was a wide-rimmed stone bowl with weird inscriptions carved into it. Then there were several packages of powders. Then a bottle of water (at least it looked like water to Jack—though from its later effects of flesh it may have been an acid.)

While Tracy's parents waited expectantly, Mr. Sykes mixed the powders and water in the bowl, stirring them with a carved bone spoon. Occasionally, he stopped stirring and tugged reflectively on his blonde beard, or scratched behind his left ear. Once or twice he spit into the mixture and whispered more horrible words over it. At a point, Mr. Sykes produced a large live toad from his bag. The toad squirmed in protest, but at the end of it all, it went into the stone bowl whole and still alive . . . and it seemed to dissolve in the strange mixture already brewing in there. When the sputtering creature's bones appeared through its melting flesh, Mildred gasped and looked sick, her face turning deathly white. Then the animal was gone, its entrails floating defiantly on the surface of the liquid for a few seconds before they too became a part of it.

More spells. More spit. More beard tugging.

Finally the bowl was filled to the brim with a red mixture. It wasn't blood, but looked just as upsetting; possibly because it was the exact same shade of crimson as its arcane maker's suit. In addition, as if the spirit of the dead toad was protesting its demise, the horrible brew was bubbling.

On the bed, Tracy began to look really worried. "Nooo!" she moaned, but her voice was almost inaudible.

Mr. Sykes smiled coldly at the possessed girl. "It's about time you left her, Cali."

Tracy looked even more upset.

Mr. Sykes now got out a paintbrush from his equipment bag. Then he got down on his knees and, using the red mixture in the stone bowl as paint, drew a circle on the floor around the bed. He took his time with the drawing/painting, once or twice pausing to ensure the lines were curved enough. The circle he drew was a large one with about two feet of clearance around each bedpost.

Finally, he got up. After checking out his work for flaws, he put the paintbrush away.

"We're almost ready," he said with satisfaction in his voice; then added in amusement: "I can just imagine what the cops would think if they walked in here now: Me, I'd go to jail forever, while you two— her parents—you'll make the morning papers."

"Let's get on with it, please," Mildred pleaded. "I can't take much more of this."

William didn't comment. Watching that still-living toad dissolve had affected him more than a little. While he accepted that the end justified the means; some things were simply to atrocious to behold. He felt somewhat dizzy and he didn't trust himself not to scream at Mr. Sykes or collapse in a faint.

Mr. Sykes nodded to Mildred, then, carrying the stone bowl with the rest of the mixture, he stepped over the red circle he'd just drawn on the floor. He was muttering something as he crossed over into it, the results of which were immediate. The circle caught fire and began burning.

Mildred Bannering immediately fainted, slumping to the floor before her husband could stop her.

William looked helplessly at Mr. Sykes. Inside the flaming ring of fire, the exorcist was drawing weird symbols on Tracy's naked body with the rest of the red mixture, while she growled like an animal and spat at him. Her fingers hooked into claws, but something was holding her flat on the bed so she couldn't reach Mr. Sykes and claw his eyes out like her own eyes clearly revealed her wish to do.

Mr. Sykes turned to stare at William. "Leave your wife there. She'll be okay. Come over here. Stand on the other side of me. Focus on your daughter. But whatever you do, don't step inside this red circle."

William gulped and moved over to where he'd been directed, standing outside the flames, which now slowly lowered and extinguished themselves.

Mr. Sykes began chanting again. Tracy immediately began flailing her body again, thrashing about on the bed like crazy. With a cold grin on his painted face, Mr. Sykes intensified his prayer or spell.

Once again, a dark jelly exited Tracy's mouth. This time, however, the jelly didn't evaporate. Instead, it hung in the air over its teenaged host, twisting and coiling like a snake. Occasionally, it congealed into the similarity of a woman's face—an incredibly beautiful but also incredibly evil female face. The face ignored Mr. Sykes. It looked instead at William with sadness and desire, promising him all the delights of Heaven here on Earth if he'd help her, if he'd just stop Mr. Sykes from tormenting her so.

William almost gave in and crossed into the red circle.

"No, it's a trick!" Mr. Sykes warned him, throwing him a glance that seemed almost psychokinetic in the way it flung him several steps backward.

The face in the black twisted up in rage and dissolved away again. The black goo resumed swirling madly over Tracy. It reached down tentacles at her, but continually struck an invisible wall over the girl's body.

Beneath the rolling and coiling black mass, Tracy lay terrified. She'd seen the face in the blackness and realized what she'd been carrying inside her. Now, each time the succubus's evil essence descended to reach her, Tracy squirmed and did everything possible to evade it.

William, thinking his heart would stop from the tension, watched the exorcist pull his daughter off the bed, then step back out of the circle.

Mr. Sykes laid Tracy on the floor, where she immediately began weeping. Then he stepped back inside the circle and made the sign of a pentagram in the air.

Next thing, the black goop dropped right down onto the bed. It squirmed there for a few seconds then was absorbed into the bed. Then the bed shook for few seconds, with all four bedposts leaping several inches off the floor. Then all was silent.

"That's done then," Mr. Sykes told William Bannering. The man was sweating through his white-paint mask; even his blonde beard seemed wet. "So long as you follow the instructions I'm about to give you, your daughter will remain free."

William looked over at his daughter Tracy, who'd now gotten over her terror and was trying to rouse her mother from her faint, then nodded at Mr. Sykes, tears of gratitude streaming down his cheeks.

***

Tracy Bannering had no more troubles after that. Once more she returned to school, where she graduated top of her class with honors. She went to university and fulfilled her dream of becoming a neurosurgeon. She got married and had children and had a happy life without a single major tragedy to mar it.

And all William Bannering found he had to do in return was to keep that north bedroom door locked, and thus the demoness caged within.

Mr. Sykes had told him: "The demoness—Cali—is now in the bed. And she'll remain trapped there."

"Can she get out?"

"Not without outside help. She'll need someone—a man—to first cross the toad-line and to fall asleep on the bed. Once he sleeps, she'll seduce him in his dreams and feed on his semen. Once he steps back over the toad-line, she'll be free again. And then she might—there's no guarantees where spirits are concerned—come looking for Tracy again."

"How about if I just burn the bed?"

Mr. Sykes had scowled. "I'm not sure. Destroying the bed may prove counterproductive. Because of the red ring, the act should result in returning Cali to Hell. But then it might not and your daughter may once again be endangered."

Then the exorcist had scowled. "Look, William, I'll level with you on this. Here's what *should* happen: Yes, the red ring on the floor *should* keep Cali locked inside no matter what; and yes, burning the bed *should* send her back to the infernal realms. But see, if you take that approach, you'll have two problems: First: how are you going to burn the bed up there in that bedroom" (they'd been sitting downstairs in the living room) "without setting your entire house ablaze; or even, if you could prevent that from happening, without the fire service arriving to put the flames out? And second: even assuming you can get those figured out, you can't step across the red line. The moment you do, Cali will be onto you like glue. And then . . . your worst nightmares will resume. So take my advice, William: Just keep the door locked and keep out of harm's way."

William had gulped. "Don't worry, no one'll get into that room from now on.

And he'd kept his word. No one *had* entered that north bedroom for the next forty years. Not until Jack Crannson had bought the house.

***

There was more, Jack discovered. Stuff that even Mr. Sykes hadn't known. Stuff which, truth be told, the trapped Cali herself hadn't had an inkling of for almost two decades:

The thing was, the spell that had locked Cali in the bed gave her time to think. Most demons are too busy doing evil to use their brains much. But now, unable to flit from sleeping man to sleeping man, Cali pondered on her current straits. At first, her only desire was to escape her prison and if she couldn't repossess Tracy Bannering, at least return to Hell. But after a long time had passed, Cali, at the point where her rage and hunger was at its most intense, suddenly realized that she didn't have to return home if she didn't want to. Using her trap as a stepping stone, she could actually exit the ether into the human world.

"I can be flesh and blood too!" she'd squealed with delight. "All I need is the right man. But Bannering isn't that man."

Bannering wasn't. She could sense in his mind that he had zero intent of entering her room. She could feel his fear each time he stared at the north bedroom door. So it would have to be someone else. Someone who had no direct experience with her. That might take a while though. She resigned herself to a long wait.

After that, everything became a waiting game. Because if Cali knew one thing about humans, it was that they grew old and died. While demons lived forever. Sooner or later, Bannering would die . . . and someone else would own this house . . .

And so the years passed . . . 20, 30, 40 . . .

And then, one pleasant spring day Jack had turned up at Cali's front door.

***

And so it was that Jack discovered to his horror that Cali had lied about how she'd gotten into the bed. It hadn't been the accident she'd claimed; but rather the result of her own callousness and greed. In her feeding frenzy, Cali had pushed her teenage host/victim into more and more self-destructive behavior, until her greed had proved her undoing.

Still, Jack didn't see how any of this knowledge helped him. He was her prisoner, her captive in his own house. *All she need do to kill me is to fuck me! And though I hate her now, my body doesn't. If she comes in her and strokes me, I'll harden instantly and . . .*

There was more to see, however. Images flooded his mind. This final scene was a recent one, with William Bannering now the old man Jack recognized:

***

William Bannering stood inside the north bedroom in his pajamas. It was about 2 a.m. He'd been unable to sleep and after a lot of consideration had wound up in here.

William Bannering was a decent and a conscientious man. And so, now that he was about to vacate his house to go live with his daughter, he didn't want to leave its future occupants the kind of curse he'd had to deal with.

106

Forty years, he thought, *that's a hell of a long time to guard something.*

Truth be told, he was tired of the task he'd been entrusted with. But he'd had no choice. Tracy's welfare had depended on it. Maybe it still did.

One thing William knew for certain was that the bed was still dangerous. The red line around it was buried beneath four decades worth of undisturbed dust. The danger seemed quiescent—the bed just another 70's relic. But, even standing where he was (three feet back from where he imagined the red circle to be) William Bannering could sense the thing he'd helped cage inside the bed pleading to be set free. He sensed Cali calling seductively to him, stroking his mind with her fingers, urging him forward. All he had to do was step over the red line, that was all. And then he'd surrender himself to her protection and fall asleep in her bed and she'd . . .

Shuddering, William stepped backward instead. He stopped retreating only when his back touched the wall.

The mental seduction died in a spurt of frustrated rage. William relaxed and pondered his intention.

He planned on burning the evil bed. In his right hand he held a can of lighter fluid; in his left a lighter.

William Bannering stood by himself in the room and had a bit of a laugh. Surely burning down the bed couldn't do that much damage anymore?

This was forty years later, after all. Tracy was fifty-five years old now, married and fat and stolid with middle age; decades distant from the angsty teen who'd held a séance with her equally green friends. He doubted the succubus would desire to invade Tracy now; she'd prefer a young nubile woman, not a filled-out matron who (if Tracy's husband Dave was to be believed) now regarded sex as a marital obligation to be endured rather than as fun.

And me? He laughed. He figured he could cross the red line without the slightest worry. At the age of seventy-eight, the last time William had had an erection was three years ago. *Even visiting me in my dreams, the damn succubus will have to bring Viagra along with her.*

So William could burn the bed down. Douse it with the lighter fluid, ignite it and get the hell out. If the entire building went up in flames, so be it then. He didn't know if he could be charged with arson for burning down his own house, but even if he was, at his age he didn't really see anyone sending him to prison. And he honestly didn't need the money he'd get from selling this place anyway. Tracy was stinking rich now. She and Dave had a monster of a home down there in Florida—a mansion with rooms to spare. And they'd been hounding him for years to give up this old place and come live with them and his granddaughter Kate.

But still, jokes aside, there was always a margin for error. William considered carefully. Mr. Sykes was long dead now, but the exorcist's words resounded down the years like bells: "And then . . . your worst nightmares will resume . . . take my advice . . . keep that door locked and keep out of harm's way."

What if . . . ? Just, what if . . . ?

So in the end, William Bannering had decided to stay safe. He'd not burnt the bed. Even though right at the end he'd again felt the spirit inside that same bed *begging* him to cross that red line and lie down on it and sleep deeply.

What he'd done instead, was to secure the lighter fluid and lighter safely in the bottom dresser drawer . . . just in case he later changed his mind. He still had at least a week before he'd be vacating the premises for good and moving over to his cousin Andy's place.

After that, feeling himself getting the start of an erection, he'd hastily reversed out of the room and locked the door behind him.

That was real close, he'd thought nervously, while crossing the hallway back to his bedroom. *I really may have to come back up here and burn that damn bed.*

But William Bannering had never returned to that room again.

***

The visions ended there, Cali entered the room then and sat on the bed. She was carrying a bottle of white wine. She sipped from the bottle and stroked Jack's cheek. "I just came to ensure you aren't feeling lonely," she said. "Would like a drink?"

He considered her face warily before responding. Was she horny again?

"Alright," he said slowly, "but no sex or I'm gonna die?"

She laughed as she tipped the bottle to his lips. "Lighten up, Jack, you aren't going to die. And me? At the moment, I'm not hungry. I just ate the pizza guy."

PART 2
SAMANTHA

CHAPTER 26

Samantha . . . Saturday night (around 10 p.m.)

Samantha Crannson was a compact, athletic woman, with short blonde hair and pale piercing eyes. She was thirty-six years old and very attractive. As required by her job, she was calm, well-organized and efficient. Her current clothing—dark slacks, long-sleeved white shirt, brown low-heeled shoes—reflected this. She had one gun in her glove compartment and a second one in a secret compartment in one of the suitcases in the rear of her Toyota Prius.

At the moment, Samantha felt very bothered as she drove her car into Bridgeport. Her most recent investigation successfully wrapped up, she was arriving in town from the southwest, along I-79.

Samantha had been calling her husband's phones—both the house landline and his mobile—all day long without any response. She'd left four voicemail messages for him and he'd not called her back. Which was very unlike Jack. Usually in their relationship, the reverse was the case: he railed at *her* for leaving her phone off while working.

"What if I've an emergency?" he'd ask. Samantha had never seen the point of the question. Only now she did. Jack did have an emergency.

She turned onto East Main Street. The cell phone video Robin had sent her still played in her mind. Her husband on the town sidewalk, ranting at the air and gesturing with his hands like he had company.

At one point she'd managed to read his lips. "I wish you'd stay away from me" he'd said, and later "You evil witch—she could have killed him with that damn chair."

It had made grim viewing. Samantha still couldn't' get her head around what she'd seen. Jack holding conversations with imaginary adversaries. Jack going crazy? It was almost inconceivable, and yet, considering his workload at the architectural firm he owned (and how he continually refused to delegate responsibility for even minor projects), it was all too possible that sooner or later he'd suffer some kind of nervous collapse.

Just like me, she thought. *It's a wonder I've not suffered a nervous breakdown. I work an even crazier schedule than he does.*

The thing was, Samantha felt she couldn't just become a stay-at-home-mom like her friend Robin and let Jack take care of her. Samantha *loved* working. For her, working, i.e. being busy in some financially productive endeavor, seemed to be the very point of human existence. She knew if she became a housewife she'd quickly expire from boredom. Samantha *loved* feeling useful to others. Not just to one man and his two or three children, but to the public at large.

Her choice of job reflected this. As a private investigator, she was able to make a difference in people's lives. Maybe a small difference overall, but a huge one to the client, who'd most times given up on getting results though the police channels.

***

Take this case she'd just wrapped up, for instance: Mary Seibert, 14-years-old. Mary had vanished from her Chicopee, Massachusetts home a month ago, reportedly after chatting on social media with a boy up in Connecticut. The Connecticut police had been to the boy's house. He'd said he'd not seen Mary: she'd told him she was heading west. He showed the police her Facebook message confirming this. Long story short, the trail had run dead. The cops couldn't find the missing girl.

Desperate, her parents had turned to Samantha for help. After following a whole lot of false trails, Samantha had finally located young Mary Seibert 'right next door' on a Kentucky farm. The girl had dyed her blonde hair red, taken to wearing glasses, and told the family she was living with, both that she was seventeen (she was large-bodied), and that she was fleeing an abusive boyfriend. Samantha had called the state cops and let them return the runaway home.

Why Mary had run away? She'd said she'd just gotten tired of living in the city and wanted to enjoy the country lifestyle for a while.

***

So Samantha enjoyed her work. In Mary Seibert's case, for instance, she couldn't get over the joy she'd seen on the girl's parent's faces when she'd linked them up for a video chat with their daughter.

And the pay was good. Worth it when one wasn't getting shot at, which *had* happened to her on several occasions.

But, doing such a job means hardly ever being home. I'm like a soldier in service—I go wherever the job takes me, no questions asked. Unfortunately, I'm married, so Jack's asking questions.

She scowled and hit the steering wheel, blaring the horn into the night though she was alone on the road. *Shit, just go ahead and admit it: Samantha Crannson, you're just as bad a workaholic as your husband is, and now . . . When last did you have sex with him? When last did you even feel in the mood to have sex with him? Both of us lying there in the dark, together, but torn apart by our selfish desires . . . each of us set on having as much of what WE WANT as we can. Neither of us thinking of the other's needs—always putting ourselves first.* She sighed miserably. *Both of us lonely as hell and yet unwilling to take refuge in each other. We're riding the rollercoaster to its logical conclusion. Shit, I hope Jack hasn't cracked up! Baby don't crack up—I love you.*

That was the real problem here: Samantha still loved her husband. And she suspected he loved her too. Right now, she was mentally kicking herself for not cutting short her search for Mary Seibert when she'd gotten that voicemail from Jack telling her that he felt ill and needed her to drive him to a hospital.

True, her lack of response wasn't entirely her fault—though sent on Monday, she'd only noticed the message on Wednesday—but since then she'd still been too busy to drive back home.

But she'd done what she could. She'd called Atwood Engineering and asked about Jack. His secretary had replied that he'd not been in that week. Apparently he had the flu and a private nurse had been hired to look after him.

That had proven a relief to Samantha. She still couldn't get Jack on the phone, but at least he wasn't dead or in the asylum. So it *was* just overwork then.

But maybe not. Samantha, her private-investigator mind sharpened by over a decade of sifting through scraps of evidence, couldn't help but feel odd.

Why? Well, firstly, even if Jack couldn't make to the phone when she called, she expected the nurse to answer the phone on his behalf. So why wasn't she doing so? And secondly, Samantha had asked Robin to drive over to the new house and make certain Jack was alright, but Robin had been weirdly reticent to do anything. Robin had come up with all sorts of excuses for not visiting Jack, till at last Samantha had angrily told her to "Forget it, then," and hung up.

Yeah, that phone call with Robin should have alerted me that something was up. She kept acting like she knew something worrying that she just didn't want to say. And since yesterday—all through today, I can't get either she or Jerry on the telephone. Anyhow, I'll find out quickly enough what the matter is. Oh heck—I just hope my husband is fine.

***

Samantha stopped at Price Cutter for some groceries. She was impatient to arrive home, but yet felt she had no choice. Still, she felt really guilty as she parked the car and got out. Was this merely more evidence of her workaholism? Of her putting her personal desires before Jack's desires even when he might need her by his side?

Samantha didn't think so. She argued to herself that despite her hurry, stopping here now was the right thing to do. Her reasoning was simple: Jack never bought anything, and she was sure that at a time like this, there'd be a need for food and possibly toiletries in the house.

With these thoughts in mind, she locked her car, crossed the asphalt parking lot and into the automatic opening of the supermarket's glass doors.

As she headed over to where the shopping carts waited, her brow creased up in thought for a moment. There was the slight chance that Jack's nurse may have gone shopping for him. Samantha quickly rejected that possibility. *Oh no, she won't have. A woman who won't even answer the damn phone? I'm gonna have some serious words with that nurse when I meet her. And depending on her reply, I might call her agency and ask for a re—*

Samantha had just been struck by an oddity. There were very few shoppers in Price Cutter at this time of night, which was normal enough. But the shoppers who were in the store all struck her as odd. While rolling her shopping cart down the aisles and loading cereal and toilet paper and cheese and soap and butter and bread and assorted drinks into it, Samantha kept having the disturbing feeling that there was something really strange about those who passed her by. Face after face after face, male and female, each one of them perfectly normal, each of them inexplicably odd in some way.

It wasn't until she stood at the checkout counter and had time to properly process her observations, that Samantha realized what looked so weird about the other Price Cutter shoppers:

The men all looked drained in some way. The women seemed normal enough, and Samantha quickly understood that she'd been projecting the male weirdness on them too.

But the men: It was really bizarre, Samantha knew and she had no explanation (and heaven knew it might be just an impression created by her own overworked mind), but . . .

Take the cashier attending to her, for instance. "Akeem," his name tag labelled him. Akeem was in his thirties and good-looking to a degree. Though smiling as he scanned and bagged her purchases, he had the expected kind of 'tired look' on his face that one would expect from someone who'd been on his feet for six hours straight.

Now, that sort of tiredness was to be expected. But, besides this, Akeem also seemed somehow 'less' than he should be.

Samantha, despite never having met this man before in her life, was nonetheless struck by the impression that this wasn't how Akeem had looked a week ago. 'Something' had leeched this Arab gentleman of his essence. (She simultaneously realized that tonight she was at the mercy of inexplicable 'somethings.')

While Akeem the cashier swiped her credit card, she examined the faces of the other shoppers beside the cash registers. Yes, she was right, all the men currently in Price Cutter had that same drained look to them. They looked alright, happy and chatting, or bored and gloomy, but laid over that, they all looked ill, though not the sort of 'ill' that would put one in the hospital. At least not immediately. Each man looked like he had a wasting illness, something like old-time tuberculosis, the sort of ailment that withered one away a little bit at a time.

It was creepy as hell though. Samantha was quite scared when she exited the supermarket and crossed to the parking lot with her shopping bags in hand.

She felt relieved to drive away from there. It didn't get much better though. All the way to the house, she slowed whenever she saw a man walking on the sidewalk, or just standing motionless. She watched their faces, saw that all of them had that same 'drained' look to them.

A fear struck her: *Oh, shit, I hope there hasn't been a chemical spill at the Anmoore Union Carbide plant, like they had in India a few years ago.*

Samantha Crannson considered her concerns well justified: Anmoore lay just two miles outside of Bridgeport, to the town's immediate southwest. Any spillage of dangerous toxins down there would be certain to have an effect up here.

But then she nixed the thought. *If that's the reason, why is it that it's just the men I'm passing who're affected by the strange blight? Yeah, and besides, if it was a UCAR problem it would be in the news.*

With no answer to her mental queries and a pile of mounting worries, she reached Maple Lake Road and pulled up the house. She felt relieved on seeing that the house lights were on.

CHAPTER 27

Cass and Laney

"It's been five days now since Dray vanished," Laney said. "Man, we gotta do something about it."

Caspar had just gotten in from work. "Do what? We've already reported to the cops. He's on their missing persons list . . . and everyone we know is looking for him." He shucked off his clothes and stepped into her bathroom.

Laney got off her bed and stood in the bathroom door. "You know what I mean. We know *who's* got him; you just don't wanna admit it."

Caspar had been about to turn on the shower, but now, turning to stare at Laney, who being at home only had her panties and bra on, he began grinning instead. Laney saw him grinning at her, looked down, and saw his stiffening penis. She realized the mistake she'd made by following him to the bathroom.

"Oh, hell no, you don't," she said, backing away with her hands raised in protest.

"Too late," Caspar said following her out of the bathroom. "Besides, I really need you. We haven't done it since Dray went missing."

"I don't feel like doing it now," Laney objected. But since she'd backed up to the bed, she had nowhere to go. A soft push was all it took to topple her backwards on the bed. Next thing she knew, her panties were being slipped off and her legs spread wide. She relaxed. Arguing was pointless. And she intended to get her point home. As Caspar's erection filled her vagina, she moaned in content. She quickly juiced up around him. She wanted him too—it was just her worries. He slipped her bra up to expose her breasts.

"Wait, let me take it off."

His eyes full of need for her, Caspar waited until Laney flung the brassiere aside, then he began moving slowly inside her.

She relaxed and enjoyed the sex, loving how he seemed to fill her to the brim with each thrust. She leaned up and kissed him. Caspar's strokes became faster and faster, as did her own moans. Finally, they came within a few seconds of each other.

Sated, calmed by their climaxes, they lay side by side on Laney's bed.

"I'm worried too," Caspar said after a while. "There's no doubt that something's happened to your brother. Where the hell can he be?"

Laney leaned up on her elbow, so her face shadowed his. "Cass, stop beating about the bush. We both know where he is."

He rolled his head on her pillow, feeling lazy and tired, reflecting how he hardly ever spent any time in his own room. Somehow he was always here in hers. He stared up at her face. Pretty, worried, and with her straw-blonde hair a little disarrayed in the aftermath of their lovemaking. "Baby, we can't prove Dray's over at Mr. Crannson's place. Yes, he might have gone over there for something, but Ms. Cali told us he left."

"What was he doing there in the first place?"

Caspar shrugged. "He's a love-struck virgin?"

Laney scowled down at her boyfriend. "I'm not buying that Cass. Yes, he went over there to see her and she didn't let him out again. She's keeping him in there."

Caspar sat up in bed and stared at Laney. "Is that what you really think? Laney, you can't be serious. You'd be making more sense if you suggested she'd tied weights to him and drowned him in the lake."

She frowned, her lower lip trembling with her emotion. "I am serious, Cass. I can't shake the feeling that that woman—Cali—has done something horrible to my brother."

She meant what she was saying. Ever since Dray hadn't come home on Wednesday, her mind had been in a ferment, aboil with nasty possibilities. With that unspoken connection some siblings had, Laney knew Dray was in big trouble. She didn't think he was dead—she was certain she'd have felt it if he was—but . . .

Caspar frowned. "But . . . the cops have already been over there. Ms. Cali told them Dray wasn't there. They told us they were satisfied she was telling them the truth."

Laney wasn't to be dissuaded from her suspicions however. "The bitch probably just flashed her tits at them and blew their minds."

"Baby, lighten up. The cops said Ms. Cali even invited them into the house to have a look around for Dray. They saw no sign of him in there."

"I just told you—she most likely met them naked at the front door. They wouldn't be thinking of anything else after that—not with those huge breasts of hers. They look like watermelons—like one of Dray's porno sluts."

Caspar didn't argue with that. He recalled how great Ms. Cali's breasts were. The memory began giving him an erection. Wincing, he dropped a hand to cover his stiffening penis. Laney would kill him if she thought he was getting hard because of the neighbor lady again.

Thankfully, Laney was too worried to notice.

"Alright," he said. "Assuming Dray *is* over there, where's his bike?"

Laney looked like she'd get angry with him. "Cass, if *you* kidnapped Dray, would you leave the evidence lying around?"

He frowned. "No, I wouldn't. I'd . . . I'd dump it in the lake." He didn't want to admit it to Laney, but to a large degree he agreed with her suspicions.

Laney wasn't mentioning it, but two days ago, when the two policemen had spoken to them after walking down the road to interview Ms. Cali, there'd been something weird about the way they'd been looking.

Two strange things actually. Firstly, both men had looked a bit drained. And secondly, they'd had this distracted and glazed look in their eyes, like they they'd been doped up.

Caspar knew the cops hadn't looked like that before going to Mr. Crannson's house. So, he couldn't discount Laney's theory. Laney had also said afterwards that the cops had sounded like they were reciting from a script.

He also recalled his own first encounter with Ms. Cali, where she'd seemingly vanished. But disappearances and mind control?

Meanwhile, Laney was staring at him. "Cass, say something! What are we gonna do?"

He bent over and kissed her, then got out of bed. "Get dressed. It's night now, a good time to head over to Mr. Crannson's house and have a look in through the windows. If there's no one home, we might even get into the house."

A grim smile on her face, Laney followed him down off the bed. "Good, that's exactly what I wanted to hear. And, we'll film whatever we find as evidence."

After Caspar's insistence that they needed to wear black clothes and sneakers, he and Laney began dressing for the night's surveillance excursion.

CHAPTER 28

Robin . . . Last Night

Last night, Robin Thurgood's sleep had been plagued with nightmares. Horrible dreams in which she was being juggled by devils. The ruthless, pitiless devils juggled her along with large spiked balls that peeled the flesh from her bones each time they touched.

She was cast up and caught ceaselessly, then tossed higher and higher. Up, down; up and down again, over and over until her head spun.

Finally, Robin woke up covered in sweat. She lay there with her eyes shut, trembling and perspiring fiercely, so weak she found it impossible to move a single muscle. The dream seemed to continue even now that she was awake, reluctant to release her from its clutches, her body moving up and down spastically, while her demonic tormentors howled with frustration as she escaped from them.

Robin was so terrified by what she'd dreamt—it had been incredibly vivid—that at first she didn't realize what had woken her up.

Then she did. Hell no, she wasn't dreaming it—the bed actually *was* moving. Bumping up and down faster and faster. She was being jerked by its motion. And in addition there were noises—both bed creaks and . . .

She opened her eyes and looked over at her husband.

What the hell is going on here?

Jerry was having sex. Right there in bed beside her, he was fucking another woman. He lay on his back and a dark-haired woman was riding him face to face. Jerry's eyes were focused on the woman's face and he was squeezing her huge breasts and all the while grinning with pleasure.

Then, in horror, Robin recognized the woman having sex with her husband. It was the woman she'd seen with Jack Crannson outside the

120

Domino's/coffee shop on East Main Street. The one who'd not shown up in the film she'd made of the pair.

A massive surge of fear ran through Robin. But how? How had she gotten into the house? They had a great home security system installed. *And how does she even know where we live anyway? And how . . . why would Jerry fuck her right here in our bed?*

Robin felt angry, but the helplessness she'd felt while being juggled in her nightmare still held her motionless. Moving even a finger took all the effort in the world.

And meanwhile, barely a foot to her left, Jerry was moaning in delight and thrusting so hard into this woman that his hips lifted clean off the bed each time, while she rode him just as intensely and laughed and laughed . . . she had a very musical laugh.

"H-h-hey!" Robin finally managed to sputter. "H-hey!"

The black-haired woman turned to look at her. "Oh, you've woken up then?"

"Wha-what are y-y-you doing here?"

The woman laughed. "I'm teaching you a lesson like I promised I would. You should have stayed out of my affairs."

"Uh . . . uh . . ." Robin fought to find an appropriate response. Something was additionally terrifying her now: the fact that even now that she and the woman were talking, her husband wasn't showing the slightest sign that he noticed she was awake, or even that she was lying there in bed beside him. Jerry wasn't looking her way at all. He was still fucking the woman as if his life depended on it.

Robin looked from her husband back to his sex partner.

The woman laughed at her confusion. "I am Cali the succubus," she explained with a gleeful grin. "No man anywhere can resist my charms." Cali leaned forward and stroked Jerry's head. He leaned up and kissed her fingers; meanwhile his fingers were buried deep in her breasts. All this while, he'd still not shown a hint that he sensed Robin beside him. Between Jerry and Cali's bodies, the fat penis vanished and reappeared, wet and slick with Cali's juices.

Cali mocked Robin: "See, I'm satisfying him like you never have before."

"Uh, uh . . ." Robin gasped. Now she understood why the video hadn't recorded this woman. *A succubus? Oh, shit.*

Cali suddenly grunted. An intense look filled her eyes and she smiled down at Robin. "I'm about to come. Watch and see what happens to your man. And tremble with terror; because your own fate will be similar to his."

At first Robin didn't understand what she meant. *Just come and get lost, bitch,* she thought. *After which I'm gonna call the cops on your ass.* She no longer believed the woman was a supernatural creature. *I'm not dreaming anymore. Once you leave here, the police are gonna arrest you for breaking and entering, you crazy—*

Cali was gasping and Jerry was gasping too. But for different reasons. Cali was clearly having a sexual climax; her eyes were dilated wide and her mouth gaped open as if she was experiencing the most intense pleasure imaginable. She stiffened and slammed her hips slowly but powerfully down on Jerry's rising crotch. Meeting him thrust for thrust. She was taking all of the cock into her pussy. She fucked him with raw intent and clear focus, getting the most sensation possible from their coupling.

Jerry, on the other hand, was gasping in pain. Robin thought she heard some pleasure also in his voice, but his enjoyment was minimal. His eyes bulged out and looked as red as if he was roaring drunk. But he wasn't drunk at all. His face was twisted up sideways in a snarl, with his lips pulled all the way back over his teeth.

He looked terrified. The way he looked terrified Robin too.

"Shit! Help, me!" Jerry howled.

Then, still thrusting away like a machine, he began shrinking. It was incredible, Robin wanted not to believe it, but she was seeing it happen. Right before her eyes, Jerry was withering away. He looked like a giant liposuction device was sucking first all the fat out of him; then all of the meat too. Almost faster than the eye could follow, his body collapsed inward. He was being reduced to mere skin and bones.

Robin pissed herself at the sight.

"Feed me, man!" Cali howled atop him. "Feed me!"

Long depressions appeared in Jerry's skin as the flesh beneath seemed to magically vanish. The skin tightened further, becoming more and more compact as the man's bones and ribs became clearly defined. His skull became a death mask. His fingers on Cali's breasts were now shrived down to the bones, their skin dry and flaking off like it was diseased.

Jerry gave a last violent thrust of his hips, groaned, "Holy shit!" then collapsed back on the bed. He twitched once or twice then lay perfectly still, staring at the ceiling with expressionless eyes.

No one needed to tell Robin that her husband was dead.

Tears rolling down her cheeks, she gasped at Cali. "You bitch! How could you? You-you-you . . ."

"Devil?" Cali finished for her. "Yes. I am a demoness." She leaned forward to kiss the corpse's withered lips, then got up off him. Jerry's penis was the only part of him that wasn't shriveled and flaking.

"Now it's time to deal with you," Cali said, licking something off her fingers. Her large breasts were coated with a layer of sweat.

Almost like magic, Robin instantly felt the weakness that had chained her to the bed draining away.

She sat up. "No!" she protested as Cali approached her. What she'd intended as a scream however, was almost inaudible.

"Your throat is still paralyzed," Cali told the frightened woman. "You're going to die quietly."

Die? Nooooo!

Robin turned to flee. She leapt down off the bed. She took two steps towards the door, but then Cali grabbed her by the neck of her nightgown. Robin turned back to fight her off. She screamed silently again.

Cali's eyes now glowed with a horrible yellow light. Her mouth was curled in a cruel smile.

"Now you will die," she said. "You will die as a lesson to others in this town who may dare to defy me."

"Please!" Robin began kicking and punching her in the face, trying to get free. She scratched Cali's face with her fingernails, pulled on her hair, and tried to head-butt her. Her fight had no effect on the succubus.

Cali just smiled evilly. Holding Robin firmly in place by the bunched neckline of her nightie, she raised a transformed hand—hairy and black with shiny black claws—and slashed down the front of the woman's body. Robin's skin parted bloodily, her right breast tearing almost completely off her chest.

Robin gaped down at the wound in horror. It spurted blood in thin jets. But she couldn't ponder her mutilation for long.

Cali's transformed hand was already back in motion. This time she plunged it deep into Robin's ribcage, grabbed hold of her heart and tore it out of her body. She held the heart up for Robin to get a good look at, then threw it away over her shoulder.

Cali stood laughing as Robin crumpled to the floor, disbelieving terror etched all over her face.

Then she vanished.

CHAPTER 29

Samantha . . . Today Again

Just as Samantha was about to stick her key in the front door, it swung open.

"Oh, hello," the woman who'd opened the door greeted Samantha. "You must be Mrs. Crannson. I'm Cali, Jack's nurse."

Samantha disliked the 'nurse' on sight. Everything about her seemed wrong.

For one thing, the woman was wrongly dressed. She wasn't wearing a uniform, but instead a pair of pink shorts and a tight tee shirt that showcased her massive breasts and seemingly stiff nipples; and she was barefoot. Then, she didn't appear professional in the least. In Samantha's experience, nurses tended to have a studious air about them; they often seemed as sterile as the hospital environments they tended to inhabit. This woman though, seemed loose, too free and easy for comfort.

This perceived laxity in the nurse's appearance and overall attitude led Samantha to her third worry: this 'Cali' woman had a definite air of the seductress to her. She gave off sexual vibes that even Samantha, who had no interest in members of her own sex, could sense. There was nothing subtle about Cali, nothing of the tease to her. The way she cocked her hip, the lustful gleam in her eye, would let men know instantly that she was on offer if they wanted her.

Samantha felt threatened by Cali's in-your-face sexiness. *And she's been here a week with my husband? When the heck did nurses begin looking like this?*

Cali stepped aside to let Samantha into the house. "Please, Mrs. Crannson, let me give you a hand with those," she said.

'Those' referred to Samantha's grocery bags. She handed them to the nurse and put her house key away again. Then, after Cali turned and walked off towards the kitchen with her purchases, Samantha stepped inside the house and looked around. At first she'd intended to return immediately to her car and fetch her suitcases from its trunk, but she'd decided that could wait for now.

I'm home, she thought. *Well, it's not really my home. Jack's made it clear that this is his place, but as his wife that means it's my place too. So . . . what?*

Samantha realized that now that she'd arrived home, she was taking her time, putting off the moment when she'd have to confront Jack and explain why it had taken her a whole week to arrive back in town when he'd clearly been really ill. She tried to think up a suitable apology. Her efforts came up short, simply because whatever she said would merely be a repeat of what she'd said the last time this kind of thing had happened.

She'd just stepped into the living room. She could hear Cali in the kitchen putting away the groceries—plate noises, cupboard noises, fridge noises. Samantha's attention however was already distracted.

She took a good look at the three men sitting in the living room, none of whom had appeared to notice her entry, then walked straight through into the kitchen to confront Cali.

"Who . . . ?" she gasped. "Who are those people watching TV in my living room?" The television sound was turned off; she'd imagined the living room was empty. Which had made the shock of seeing them all the more disturbing.

Cali put the tub of butter she was holding into the fridge, shut the door, and then straightened up to reply. "Oh, those guys? They're friends of Jack's, Mrs. Crannson."

She called him 'Jack,' not 'Mr. Crannson,' Samantha noted instantly. *That's a red flag.*

But even if Jack was screwing his nurse, that was a minor concern at the moment.

"Friends of Jack's?" Samantha asked, just managing to keep an edge of hysteria from her voice, though she could clearly hear that she'd abruptly both gotten louder and higher in pitch. "Friends of his, you say? The three of them look like concentration camp victims to me. Are they refugees from a warzone?"

It was quickly dawning on Samantha why the sight of those three men in the living room was so alarming: The three men—looking so withered one would expect them long dead and buried—suddenly struck her as being in the final stages of whatever strange affliction now had a hold on Bridgeport's menfolk. At least those she'd noticed on her drive over.

Maybe she was jumping to conclusions, but now Samantha Crannson knew for sure that a whole lot was wrong.

"Yes, those men aren't well at all," Cali agreed solemnly with her. "They're very ill."

"My eyes already told me that much," Samantha said. "What I want to know is, what the hell is wrong with them?"

"They've a rare condition called sexomiasis. It dries one up from the inside."

"Is it contagious?" Samantha asked helplessly. "I've never heard of it before."

Her companion laughed. Samantha noted how musical her laugh was. Perfectly matching the woman's exceptional beauty. "Not really," she replied afterwards. "So long as you don't sleep with them."

"Ugh," Samantha said. "It's an STD then?"

"But don't worry about it," Cali added without interest. "Jack hasn't caught it from them. Look, forget those guys. They're incurable—as bad as vegetables now. The only thing that gets any kind of a reaction from them is the TV; they can watch it for hours. Of course, one needs to be careful with sexomiasis patients: one sight of a pretty girl and they all pull their cocks out and start wanking. Last time they came all over your coffee table and I had to wipe that shit off of there. Ugh, just disgusting."

Samantha managed to overlook Cali's sudden switch to vulgarity. "How the hell did they get here?"

Cali smiled. "I already told you that, Mrs. Crannson. They came to visit your husband."

"In that condition? Girl, those three guys don't look like they could find their way to the toilet if it was right in front of them." Samantha wasn't buying any of this anymore. Something here was fucked up big time. First in the town itself, and now in her own house. She decided to backtrack outside to her car and fetch the gun in the glove compartment. Yes, that was the right thing to do. Before . . .

Samantha was about to open her mouth to make the excuse to Cali that she'd forgotten something in her car that she needed to go fetch, when she felt a gentle 'touch' of persuasion on her mind. Just the barest of touches that made her receptive to the nurse's next words:

"But, of course, it's high time we went upstairs to visit Jack, Mrs. Crannson."

"Call me Sam, please."

"Okay, Sam . . . please accompany me upstairs. Your husband has been desperate to see you."

Feeling weird and yet unable to resist the nurse's suggestion, Samantha followed Cali out of the kitchen. Before ascending the stairs she did her best to not look at the three withered men who sat staring at the living room TV.

At the top of the stairs Samantha turned right.

"No, the other way," Cali redirected her with a firm hand on her forearm.

Samantha pointed in surprise. "But Jack's—our—bedroom is that way."

"The north bedroom has qualities that your husband finds particularly endearing," Cali said. "Since falling ill, he's moved in there. He's really attached to it now."

"Oh." So they went left instead.

As Cali led the way forward, Samantha finally couldn't resist the question: "Hey, Cali, you're a nurse. Don't you have a uniform?"

Cali paused with her hand on the door to the north bedroom. "Oh, I do, Sam, but this is modern home therapy. The experts believe casualwear puts the patient in a better frame of mind, helps him recover faster."

Samantha paused in pondering what the red glow spilling under the bedroom door was, to ask one more question: "Okay, I get that, but do the experts have any problems with you wearing a bra?"

Cali laughed. "Wow, Sam, you're even funnier than Jack said you were."

"I'm *not* joking," Samantha said through gritted teeth. "For a nurse, you dress more like a hooker." Oh, how she disliked this slut.

"You're jealous then?" Cali asked mockingly. "You're angry that my body is better than yours?"

Samantha was angered by her impudence, but, before she could reply, Cali had pushed the bedroom door open and pulled her inside the room.

"Oh my God!" Samantha gasped in horror once she saw Jack on the bed.

Samantha hurried over to the bed and gaped down at Jack. "Darling, darling, what happened to you!?"

"*I* happened," Cali said behind her. "Welcome home, Mrs. Crannson . . . oh, I mean, 'Sam.' "

Samantha didn't turn around. She was standing inside the glowing red circle around the bed, which she'd deduced was the source of the light that had been spilling under the door.

"Jack! Jack! What on earth happened to you?" He looked just like the men downstairs. Not as far gone, but surely he'd soon be in exactly the same shriveled state as those three sufferers were.

"Sam, I told you that *I* happened to your husband," Cali repeated, her tinkling laughter filling the bedroom. "He's all *mine* now, and so are *you* too, dear, for your information."

CHAPTER 30

Caspar and Laney

"Shush!" They'd both stopped at the sound of the car pulling up into the driveway. Then Caspar had padded around the side of Mr. Crannson's house to see who the new arrival was. It had been a woman. Caspar had watched her unload shopping bags from her car and head towards the house. He listened to Cali admit the woman into the house, then quietly returned to Laney's side.

"Who was it?" she whispered.

"Mrs. Crannson."

"How'd you know for sure?"

"Ms. Cali mentioned her name when she let her in the house."

"Good, that means she's occupied now. Let's get on with the search."

They parted the window drapes and Caspar peeked inside. This room seemed to be a study; along with a good number of books, the room also contained a steel and glass drafting table, with a hinged lamp bent over it. On a second table sat a slim laptop beside which lay several scrolled-up bundles that Caspar assumed were building plans. On a wall bench sat four small models of houses and a three-foot-wide to-scale representation of a shopping mall.

Caspar leaned back out. "Nothing in there," he said. "I think it's his office."

"Let me make sure," Laney said, pulling him out of the way. Shorter, she couldn't lean as far in as Caspar, so he lifted her up a bit.

"Alright," she agreed, a moment later, "next window."

This was the second room they'd looked into. The first had been empty, filled with boxes Mr. Crannson hadn't yet unpacked.

Caspar had on black jeans and a black hoodie which actually belonged to Dray. Laney was dressed in black leather pants, a black tee shirt, and had covered her blonde hair with a black scarf. So long as the pair kept close to the house and didn't make much noise, they could easily be mistaken for shadows by anyone who walked past. Not that they expected anyone would show up; they were at the rear of the house.

To aid their search, Caspar had a small flashlight on him, for rooms like the first one, where the lights were off. Laney held her cellphone at the ready to record whatever evidence they might turn up.

For protection, Caspar had a switchblade, while Laney had a can of pepper spray.

The night was just right for their purposes, the sky nice and dark, the moon and stars mostly hidden by clouds.

They moved on down the line of windows. The next window was small and high off the floor. No chance in hell of Laney ever reaching up to it. Even Caspar had to stand on tip-toes to peek in.

"Not this one either," Caspar said after parting the drapes and shining his torch into the darkness.

"What's in there?" Laney asked.

"Toilet."

"Oh. That explains why it smells like shit."

They moved on. The next room lay on the opposite side of the back door. Caspar first checked the back door.

"Locked," he told Laney.

The first two windows on the other side of the door were at normal height and brightly lit. What's more, both windows were open. Their yellow drapes fluttered in the gentle night breeze.

"Kitchen," Laney immediately said. "Smell of food's a giveaway any day. Wonder what's cooking in there."

"Shush! They're in there."

They both ducked and merged with the shadows. Laney's eyes widened and she listened. She heard a voice say, "Okay, Sam . . . please accompany me upstairs. Your husband has been desperate to see you."

Next came the sound of departing footsteps. After a short wait, Laney and Caspar both straightened up and looked in the kitchen windows, one of them staring through each window.

After a brief peek, Laney shrugged and turned away. "Well, you don't really expect Dray to be in here, except he's in the fridge with the beer."

Caspar smiled. "One more room on this side and then we'll have to move round to the front of the hou—"

"Jack! Jack!" a woman moaned upstairs. "What on earth happened to you?"

Both Caspar and Laney had frozen motionless at the cry. They stood looking up at the window above them. It was shut, barred and draped, but despite all this a pinkish glow diffused through the glass. Like the escaping pink light, the woman's voice too had seemed spooky.

"Mrs. Crannson sounds real upset," Laney finally ventured.

"I don't like this at all," Caspar agreed. "Laney, let's head home and come back tomorrow."

She shook her head. "Listen—she's stopped." Meaning the upset woman upstairs had fallen silent.

Caspar listened. He could hear conversation above them, but it was muted. Apparently the only reason the wife's cry had filtered down to them had been its volume.

Laney tugged on Caspar's sleeve. "Come, baby, let's get on with it." Then seeing his reluctance to follow her, she added, "Maybe Jack's the name of her dog. You know how some people can get about pets."

"Jack is her *husband's* name. Something is wrong with him; that's why she screamed like that."

She frowned at him. "So what, huh? You're leaving? Cass, I need to find my elder brother!" Her eyes were cold, set with determination.

Caspar sighed. He knew Laney. No matter how dangerous the situation now, she wasn't about to leave even if he did.

He regarded the stubborn set of her lips. Then he bent and kissed her on them. "Nah, we can't head home before we've determined if Dray's here in this house or not." He grinned at her. "Come on, girl. Let's check the next window."

They hurried towards it.

CHAPTER 31

Samantha, Cali, & Jack

"What the hell have you done to my husband?" Samantha asked Cali coldly, her patience at breaking pitch. "What have you done to Jack!?"

Cali laughed, then she gripped her breasts in both hands and squeezed them provocatively. "I only did to him what you weren't doing—I *fucked* him. The rest . . . well, I don't really like how he looks now either, but then looks aren't everything."

Samantha glowered at Cali. She was visibly simmering. She was clearly doing everything in her power to keep from charging at Cali and throttling her. Her thoughts bubbled and simmered. This hooker of a so-called 'nurse' had given Jack a disease.

She fought back the tears that came to her eyes. *Jack, I love you. Jack, I love you!*

Up till now, Cali had been standing near the bedroom door. Now she stepped over the red circle and came up to the bed. The circle glowed brighter as she crossed it.

Samantha was standing by Jack's head, stroking his hair with one hand. Jack was staring up at her pleadingly—his eyes—sunken hollows in his face—begged her to do something to help him. She wanted to help him—oh, how she wanted to help him, but, for the life or her, Samantha didn't have the foggiest idea what she could do. Jack looked, just . . .

Cali was standing beside Jack's waist. "I haven't really damaged him," she said. "Look, the best part of him still works." With that statement, she began manipulating his penis, which lay limp in his crotch.

"Stop it!" Samantha reached towards Cali, but . . . but something stopped her. Once again she felt the persuasive force that had convinced her to follow Jack's so-called nurse up the stairs. "Stop mastur—" Weakness filled her. Her stretched-out arm fell to her side again. She felt as if her feet had just been nailed to the floor. She stood there watching. "Stop it!"—she finally managed to croak. "Stop . . . you're hur-hurting hi-hi-him!"

Cali grinned mockingly. "Hurting him? Even back in the dark ages no one believed that having an erection hurt a man." She stopped moving her hand. "See?"

Samantha's gaze dropped from Cali's sneering face to Jack's crotch. Her husband had a throbbing erection. Cali gently squeezed the hard penis. A clear drop of pre-come oozed from the organ's tip. Cali lifted her hand to her mouth, spit in her palm and then returned her hand to Jack's penis. She smeared the spittle over the erect manhood (causing Jack to gasp with delight), then began stroking it up and down again.

Samantha looked from Jack's crotch to his face. The expression on his tired and lined face was a mixture of intense pleasure and even greater dread. She looked back across at Cali. "What do you want with him?"

Another evil laugh. "You forget that I'm his nurse. Sexomiasis patients need regular release, if they're to be cured."

"Cured? But you said . . ."

"I lied. I'm not really your husband's nurse—I'm a demoness."

"What?" Samantha's eyes widened at the revelation. A demoness? But there was no arguing with the truth of Cali's words. Even if Samantha had wanted to deny the other woman's claim, how could she then explain the inexplicable force that even now held her captive and a slave to Cali's will?

"Yes, I am a demoness," Cali confirmed to Samantha.

While speaking, Cali kept manipulating the stiff penis. She increased the speed of her strokes and Jack's gasps intensified. Finally semen spurted from the cock.

"Fuuuukkk!" Jack gasped as if he was dying. Then, while Samantha watched, his body shrunk a little more. Samantha was utterly horrified—it seemed like a hole had been made somewhere in her husband's skin through which his flesh was leaking out. He didn't shrivel much, but the increase in the wrinkling of his skin was noticeable. With the way he already lay bedridden, this just made him seem more like a corpse.

"Stop it!" she growled at Cali.

Cali was licking Jack's semen off her hand. "I'm already done."

"You're killing him."

"He enjoyed it. Look at his face."

Samantha looked. Jack had a look of utter rapture on his face. Samantha hadn't seen him look like that in ages. But then she'd not had sex with him in ages either. She looked back at Cali. The woman's—demoness'?—grip on her mind seemed to have loosened a little after her orgasm; she could think better, move her limbs a little.

"Look, we need to get him to a hospital," she protested.

"No," Cali said. "He stays right here in this bed with me. I like him very much. You don't like him at all, do you?"

"I love him," Samantha admitted, hating Cali for making her defend herself like this. She turned to Jack, and tears running down her face, repeated the declaration to him: "I love you, Jack. I really do. I'm sorry not to have been here for you more often."

Jack's expression had sobered up now, and she thought he had tears in his eyes too. She wished he would say something, but he seemed completely unable to voice his thoughts.

"I love him and I'm taking him to a hospital right away," she informed Cali again. "And you're not going to stop me doing so."

This time Cali did not laugh. Her expression cold as ice, she shook her head. "You can't leave here anymore. Once you stepped over that red circle on the floor, you fell completely under my control. Now you belong to me, just like your husband does. And . . ." she bit her lower lip seductively, "I'd very much advise you to behave yourself and not make me give you a demonstration of how nasty and dangerous I can be."

To make her point, Cali pointed to the still-healing wound on Jack's left thigh. Then, not bothering to wait for Samantha's reply, she sat on the edge of the bed and grinned a lascivious grin at her. "Now, sit down, woman, and cradle your husband's head while I give him a little more pleasure. Obey me. Obey your mistress!"

Samantha didn't want to obey, but that same evil force she'd felt earlier compelled her to. Almost as if she had no more control over her limbs and actions, she found herself sitting by Jack's head, then lifting his head onto her lap. At the middle of the bed, Cali had already begun stroking Jack's penis again.

While Samantha was seating herself, Cali had removed her tee shirt, freeing her breasts. Even though not fully in control of her own mind now, Samantha nevertheless couldn't help the envy she felt on seeing the demoness' breasts—big and firm and with proportionately overlarge nipples. And with his head cradled on her lap and as such tilted upwards, she knew that there was no way Jack could avoid seeing Cali's chest too. Already, Jack's penis was stiff again, and Cali was spitting down on it, preparatory to this second dose of masturbation.

This is sexual abuse, Samantha thought weakly. *And because I had a lot of groceries, I left both my gun and my cellphone downstairs in the car. Shit! What am I gonna do now? This woman—demoness, whatever—is crazy. She's dangerous!*

"Now," Cali said, when she'd gotten Samantha's attention again, "let me, as a succubus, teach you the right way to masturbate a man; lots of human females are exceptionally bad at doing so. It's simple: Firstly, after wetting your hand with some spittle, you take a firm grip on the penis around its middle and . . ."

CHAPTER 32

Cass & Laney

"There he is," Laney said. "There's Dray!"

"That?" Caspar gaped. "Laney, be serious. How in the frigging hell can that be your brother?"

Their search around Jack Crannson's residence had finally brought them to the living room windows. The windows were open and the living room lights were on, but the drapes had been shut. When they'd carefully parted the drapes, they could see everything clearly. Which is what had led to Laney's current comment.

"It's him," she repeated. "He's still got his work clothes on."

"Yeah," Caspar grudgingly agreed. Though he didn't understand how young, plumpish Drayfuss Springer could now look like a guy long overdue for a nursing home. "But how can that be him?"

Laney was insistent and convinced. "Remember how we told you what Amos Green looked like when we found him dead in the coffee shop? Well, he looked exactly like that."

Peering closely now, Caspar decided that the withered old man sitting in the living room chair and staring listlessly at the muted television did bear a passing resemblance to Dray. There were two other similarly withered old men in there both also with their eyes glued to the silent TV.

"Alright," he agreed. "That's Dray. So . . ." Watching those three men, as motionless as statues, Caspar felt frightened. He had a very good idea that he and Laney were about to step into a lake of shit. But he couldn't leave Dray in there (oh fuck, is that really Dray?), and Laney certainly wasn't about to abandon her older brother, so . . .

"We need to get him out of there," Laney confirmed with a determined look on face.

"Yeah, baby," Caspar agreed. "But how? That's the question now."

Laney had a ready answer. "Easy. We climb in the window and carry him out."

Caspar considered that. "We'll be taking a chance on triggering security alarms."

"Cass, I don't think Ms. Cali's about to call the police on us. Do you?"

"You're right. But . . . you wait outside here, and I'll climb in and pass him out to you."

"Can you handle him alone?"

Caspar pointed to 'Dray.' "On a good day, no. But at the moment, your brother looks to only weigh about a fifth of what he normally does." He shuddered. "I sure hope that what he's got ain't catching."

That said, Caspar pulled the window more fully open and climbed up onto the sill. A moment later he was inside the Crannson's living room. He gave Laney a thumbs up and stole quickly over to Dray's side.

"Come on, dude," Caspar whispered. "We gotta get you outa here."

Dray made no response. Indeed, neither Dray nor either of the other two men in the living room showed the slightest sign that they'd registered Caspar's presence in their midst. The eyes of all three withered men were riveted on the TV screen. The TV was showing an old episode of *Friends* droning on without sound.

"Come on," Caspar whispered a little louder. "We gotta go before she comes back!"

Still no response from Dray.

"What's the matter?" Laney called from the window.

Caspar hurried back over there for a quick conference. "He's not moving or doing anything. He's like a vegetable—it's like he's brain dead or something."

"Maybe his brain's withered too. Look, baby, just lift him out of the damn chair and bring him over here and lets take him home. I'm sure once he's got his video games and beer again, he'll be okay."

Caspar doubted that it would be that easy to fix Dray, but still he hurried back over to his friend's side.

"Time to leave, dude," he explained while lifting Dray out of the armchair.

Now Dray did speak. "Want teeeeeveeee," his withered lips protested. With a surprisingly quick motion of his atrophied hands, he grabbed hold of the armchair's arms to prevent himself from being moved.

Caspar felt frustrated—every additional second spent in here increased the chances of their being discovered. He was already scared shitless—the way Dray's two companions kept staring at the television screen had already put the fear of sharing a similar fate into him.

Dray, however, held tight to the chair. No matter how hard Caspar tried, he couldn't prize Dray's fingers free.

"What's the matter now?" Laney called from the window.

"Your brother doesn't want to go home."

"Hey, Dray!" Laney called. "Dude, there's beer and videogames and potato chips at home waiting for you."

Dray's head turned slowly to look at her. His leathery lips parted. "Beer? Videogames?"

Laney nodded. "Yeah, a fridge full of beer and . . . and . . . porn too. With Amy Anderson—that slut whose tits you dig so much."

A smile creased Dray's dried-up face. "Not need porn. No longer virgin. Fucked Cali."

"What?" Caspar and Laney stared at each other in shock.

"Fucked Cali real hard," Dray drawled like a slowed-down record, a dreamy look on his face. "Came inside Cali's butthole. Tiiiiightttt!"

But after that, he didn't prove any more trouble to his sister and her boyfriend. He let go of the armchair. Caspar easily carried him across to the window—Dray didn't seem to weigh much more than the bones beneath his perilously taut skin. Caspar passed him outside to Laney, who, unprepared for how little he weighed now, almost dropped him in surprise.

"Now let's get on home," Caspar said, climbing out to join them.

"Beer!" Dray agreed.

PART 3
CALI

CHAPTER 33

Cali

"You're a monster!" the wife was saying. "You're completely nasty. How can you do this to him?" There were tears in her eyes, though she was trying hard not to cry. A tough woman. Cali was familiar with the type. The sort that trivialized marital relations: the kind that made love grudgingly with their husbands. And a man without a satisfactory sex life must of necessity have sexual dreams.

Dreams that I can inhabit, the succubus thought with relish as she licked the semen from Jack's latest orgasm off her fingers. Once again he'd shrunk a little. But not too much. She needed him alive in the bed.

"You're a monster," Samantha repeated.

"It doesn't matter what you think I am. Jack loves my touch. Would you like me to demonstrate it again?"

Samantha's stare of defiance immediately turned to a pleading one. "No, please don't. Don't!"

Cali smiled at her. "Like I said, just behave yourself. At the moment, I control this town—you'll be easy to dispose of."

The wife's scared look delighted her. *Her fault anyway. If she'd spent more time in bed with her man, spreading her legs, she'd not be in her current straits. Not that I'm upset: her marital lapse meant that I got just what I needed at exactly the right time. One more year stuck in this horrible bed would have driven me crazy. Of course, I don't control the entirety of Bridgeport yet, but I will soon, and then my power will be almost limitless . . .*

CHAPTER 34

Jack

Jack listened helplessly to the vocal exchanges between his wife and the succubus. He wished he could intervene. But now Cali had drained him so much that he felt himself hanging between life and death.

Jack was scared. He couldn't stop fearing that Cali might accidentally bleed too much 'essence' from him. She wouldn't mean to do it—she needed him in this bed—but she might kill him while toying with Samantha's emotions.

Poor Sam! Jack couldn't help but feel for his wife. She loved him! Well, he loved her too.

I love you too, baby! he thought fiercely back at her. He could only think. Speech was impossible: his lips felt heavier than lead. His tongue felt dead. All he could do was think his love at her.

Think and plot a way to escape.

He looked from Samantha's tormented face to Cali's triumphant one. Cali was preening herself, adjusting her raven-black hair with her fingers and pouting. True, she was beauty personified. Oh, God, he'd never seen so gorgeous a vision—but she was also so evil that he dreaded her smile almost as much as he dreaded her touch. And he did dread her touch. Once she caressed him, even fleetingly, his body was certain to respond, and this would merely lead to the loss of more of himself.

He watched her smile, hating her and wishing there was something he could do about it.

Cali wasn't invulnerable. Since being in the bed, Jack had slowly discovered her secrets: in some ways he now knew the succubus better than she knew herself. He knew, for instance, that this bed he lay in now was the key to Cali's power . . . and that destroying it would . . . well, one couldn't actually destroy a demoness, but . . . destroying the bed would automatically pull Cali out of the human world, back into the dream world of ether and insubstantiality.

Jack blacked out for a few seconds. When he regained consciousness, he strained to recall what he'd been thinking about. In the interim little appeared to have changed between the two woman seated on the bed. He was still unable to move much more than his eyes; he still lay with his head cradled on his wife's lap; she still looked miserable; and Cali was still preening herself. Now the demoness was examining her perfect breasts for imaginary defects.

Jack finally picked up the thread of his thoughts again. Ah, yes—the second thing.

Jack also knew from his flashbacks into his evil jailor's past, that the means to destroy the bed were already in this room. Earlier, whenever Cali visited the north bedroom, Jack had had to restrain himself from staring over at the dresser, where old man Bannering had left that can of lighter fluid and the lighter the last time he'd been inside here.

Cali, however, seemed to have completely forgotten about the lighter fluid and lighter. Or perhaps she simply didn't know what they were. It was an amusing thought, but just like she'd not at first known what cellphones were, it was very possible—almost certain, actually—that most of the modern world made little sense to her.

So, if I can just get it across to Sam how to destroy this bed, we'll be free. But since I can neither move nor speak at the moment, that might take some doing, right?

It was right at this moment that Cali frowned and said to Samantha, "Hold on, I'll be back in little bit—I've something to attend to."

And then she vanished from off the bed. There was no thunderclap or flash of light. The succubus just winked out of sight.

Jack, used to such happenings, stared up at his wife to see her reaction.

Samantha's reaction was exactly what he'd expected it to be. She was gaping and pointing at the spot on the bed where Cali had been sitting, where even now the curved imprint of her fantastic buttocks was clearly visible.

"She . . . she . . . she . . . !" She gaped down at him. "She . . . she . . . !"

Oh, you ain't seen nothing yet, honey! Jack thought up at her.

CHAPTER 35

Cass & Laney

"Beer," Dray repeated, as Caspar and Laney prepared to carry him off home. There was no chance whatsoever of him walking. He was just rather unwieldy. Dray wasn't the least bit heavy, but Caspar was now worried that he might break if handled roughly.

"Yeah," Laney agreed with her brother. "There's lots of beer waiting in the fridge." She grinned and stroked his hair, though the very act of touching him in his current condition felt nauseating. Still she laughed. "And congratulations on finally losing your virginity. Was Ms. Cali any good in bed?"

"The ber-ber-best," Dray drawled. "Sh-sh-sh-sh-shit!" He swung his hand to slap Laney's.

A cold wind was blowing though the yard. Fifty yards away, down beyond the foot of the Crannson's driveway, dull moonlight reflected off the surface of Maple Lake. Then, just as abruptly as the moon had been unveiled, it was once more obscured by clouds.

Caspar was relieved. All they had left to do now was leave this crazy place. And fast too, before Ms. Cali—was she a witch, or what?—came downstairs and discovered them. He heaved Dray up over his shoulder in a fireman's carry.

But then everything went wrong. Just like that, Ms. Cali suddenly appeared out of thin air in front of them. Right in front of them, so they couldn't run off. Well they could have dashed *around* her, but there seemed to be a force stopping them from leaving her. As it was, Caspar could only stare and gulp at how beautiful she was. And her breasts; once again her breasts were on display, as large and perfect and bouncy as a young man could ever wish them to be.

"H-Hiii!" Laney yelped on seeing her. "We weren't stealing anything, honest!"

"Liar." Cali pointed to Dray. "You were stealing *him*. Don't you understand that he's mine now?"

"Here, you can have him back," Caspar said, thrusting Dray at her. "Shriveled up like this, he isn't really of any use to us at all." With Dray weighing next to nothing, it was easy to keep him held out at arm's length.

"Yeah," Laney quickly agreed with her boyfriend. "We-we-we were just taking Dray home to inflate him, then return him back to you."

"Shiiiiittt!" Dray gasped like he was being deflated some more.

Cali smiled. "How nice of you both. And how thoughtful too. I heard you mentioning beer. Would you like to share some with me?"

Caspar, who was still holding Dray out at arm's length, shook his head. "No, ma'am, we've got lots of beer at home."

"Yeah," Laney quickly added. "Too much, even. You know the kinda drunkards guys are."

"I insist," Cali told them. Then she stepped past Dray and touched Caspar's crotch. She stroked then gripped his penis. "Yes, I knew I was correct—you do have an erection." She leaned forward and kissed Caspar on the lips. "Come inside and I'll take care of it for you."

Caspar grinned stupidly at her. He knew he should be running for his life—just from seeing how Dray now looked after sleeping with this woman—but something in his head was making him want Ms. Cali more than he'd ever desired any woman in his life.

"Alright," he agreed. "Let's go."

"No, don't!" Laney yelped in horror. "Don't go with her, Cass! She'll . . she'll . . . !"

Cali turned a wolf's grin on her. "Don't be jealous, little girlfriend. You can have him back afterwards. Besides, you're coming along too."

"Nooo!" Laney gasped as the convincing force took over her brain.

"But of course, yes," Cali bent and whispered in her ear. "I do my best performing before an audience. And I'll let you share in the fun."

Next, Cali took Dray from Caspar. She stepped over to the living room window, pulled back the curtains, and then, to a gasp of horror from Laney, unceremoniously flung Dray in through the window.

There was the sound of Dray's contact with the floor, in addition to what sounded like several bones all breaking at once, and a loud yelp of "Evil bitch!" Then silence.

Cali turned back to Caspar and Laney. "Forget him. I'll put him back in his chair later. He likes those old sitcoms." She cocked her index finger at them both. "Now, follow me, both of you. Let's go and have some fun in bed. There's a nice soft one in the downstairs guestroom."

Unable to help themselves, Caspar and Laney followed after the succubus. If anything, Caspar's penis was harder now than ever before in his life.

CHAPTER 36

Samantha & Jack

Once Samantha had gotten over her shock at Cali's disappearance, she hurried across the bedroom to try the door. Jack's gun was in *his* bedroom. If she could just reach it . . .

Like a gas ring, the glowing red circle flared up in flames as she crossed it, then died down again.

"Shit!" Samantha swore on trying the door. "The bitch locked it."

She wrestled with the door handle for a while, then tried to muscle the door open. When brute force produced no effect, she calmed down and began thinking.

The windows! We're just on the second floor. I can make a rope from the sheets, then—!

She pulled back the drapes and saw the bars. Shit! again. She considered flinging the windows open and yelling for help, but Cali was certain to 'teleport' herself back into the room before any assistance would arrive. Samantha had already figured out that she and Jack's best hope in this insane situation was to somehow sneak out of the house (and possibly out of town?) before their captor realized they'd gone missing. And besides, if Cali really was as powerful as she claimed to be, and had as much control over Bridgeport as she said she did, then there was no point calling for help—all Samantha would be doing would be summoning the demoness' minions.

After a brief glance across at Jack, Samantha moved over to the dresser. She began pulling out the drawers. Nothing of use here, just some underwear that might have been in style in the 50's, and in the bottommost drawer of all, a small yellow can of barbeque lighter fluid and a new lighter. She grimaced at the two items. It would be pointless trying to burn down the door—she'd most likely set the house alight and the smoke would kill both Jack and herself before the fire service arrived.

Disgusted, Samantha shut the drawers and returned to sit beside Jack. This time too, the red circle caught fire as she crossed it.

Staring down at Jack, Samantha immediately got the idea that he was trying to tell her something. His fingers moved sideways but weren't actually pointing anywhere.

She bent and kissed his lips. "What is it, darling?" she enquired.

He kept jerking his hand sideways, like he wanted to gesture at a point in the room. He also kept opening his mouth, but the words seemingly wouldn't form on his tongue. All that emerged from his throat were grunts.

Samantha finally decided that Jack just wanted to leave the bed.

"You wanna get out of bed, darling?"

He grunted louder than before, so she figured her assumption was right.

After another kiss, this time on the forehead, she got him upright. He'd lost weight and was easy to move at her whim. Holding him close, steering his legs on the floor, she dragged Jack towards the circle to cross it.

And then the circle flared up in fire again. However, this time the flames were not the six-inch high sort that had accompanied her earlier crossing and re-crossing the red ring: these flames were four foot high tongues of dancing fire that also seemed to extend a foot outward from the ring.

Samantha instantly stepped back. Once she did so, the flames died down again. She made another attempt to step out of the ring with Jack and the flames once more rose up all round the bed. This time they were much higher, almost reaching the ceiling, though their fire didn't smoke and other than the intense heat they gave off, they did no damage to the room.

Samantha knew however, that the flames would burn herself and Jack to ash if she so much as attempted to cross through them.

She stepped back again. Once more the orange and yellow blaze died down.

Samantha returned Jack to the bed and sat beside him thinking. All that remained of the fire now were a few small flames—none higher than two inches—flickering back and forth along the red ring a foot or so from Samantha's feet. The rest of the ring remained in its usual glowing state with no fire.

Samantha got the message. "She's telling us we can't leave," she told Jack. "But the bitch is wrong. We *can* get out of here. We just need to figure out how!"

With a frown on her face, she set her mind to figuring out how to escape the red circle.

***

While Samantha spoke, Jack felt his head fill with a glowing red haze. All of a sudden he felt strength pouring into him. Cali's evil strength. His body came alive, and he found he could sit up.

Jack's first instinct was to yell out to Samantha that they needed to burn the bed. But his lips wouldn't move the way he wanted. Instead of what he had in mind to say, what came to his tongue were words of hatred for Samantha. What filled his mind was red rage and the urge to kill the woman he loved.

***

"I'm not giving up," Samantha was saying. "We're not giving in to her. Hell no! I'm gonna find a way to defeat Cali and save both our lives and this town from her influence. Because, if she wins here, who the hell knows what she'll want next. The whole state of West Virginia?"

It was then that she felt Jack sit up beside her. She whirled around in delight, but then her delight turned to horror. Because she could see in Jack's eyes that this wasn't her husband anymore. His eyes glowed with a horrible yellow light and his voice, when he spoke, was Cali's:

"I warned you," Cali said through Jack's lips. "I warned you not to mess with me. I warned you what I'd do to you." Jack laughed, but it was Cali's musical mirth emerging from his lips. "So now, you're going to die! Yes! And to show you my power, you're going to die by your own husband's hands!"

And with that statement, Jack grabbed Samantha by the throat and began strangling her.

"Stop it, baby!" she yelped at him.

But he didn't. Rather, his fingers tightened around her throat and he forced her down onto the bed and knelt on her for more leverage.

His face twisted into a grimace. "Oh, I'm really enjoying this, bitch!" Cali mocked through Jack's lips.

CHAPTER 37

Caspar, Laney, & Cali

"Oh, I'm really enjoying this, bitch!" Cali said, while Caspar and Laney followed her into the guest bedroom. She seemed to be talking to herself, and when they looked at her face, her eyes had a glaze of concentration to them.

But then she stopped talking to herself and seemed to focus all of her attention on them.

"Take your clothes off," she ordered Caspar, then grinned at Laney. "You too, darling."

"I don't want to!" Laney said.

"Of course you do," Cali said. And of course, it was true, all of a sudden Laney felt like obeying Cali. She didn't feel aroused at all—if anything, she felt both jealous and disgusted—but she understood that both she and her boyfriend had no say at all in the matter anymore. They were both Cali's sex toys now, and she could and would do with them both as she saw fit.

So Laney undressed, as quickly as she could. Caspar was already undressed; he had a goofy, expectant smile on his face. He stood there erect and proud, gripping his hard penis and waiting for Cali to remember him. Laney tried to catch his eye, but Caspar no longer seemed to know who she was. He leered at her without recognition and winked and made thrusting signs with his hips in Cali's direction.

Laney tried to hide her modesty, covering her breasts with her right forearm and her crotch with her left hand.

Cali regarded her with some amusement. "What are you so prudish about? You don't have anything that I don't."

She smiled nicely at Laney. "It's alright, girl. Take your hands away and let me see your breasts. I'm sure you've a lovely set." She turned to Caspar. "Does she have great breasts?"

He appeared to remember where he was. He grinned. "Yeah, Ms. Cali, her boobs are wonderful. Not as good as yours, of course—I mean, no woman on Earth has boobs that can compare with yours—but, yes, ma'am, Laney's boobs are first-rate too."

"Asshole," Laney muttered, but she removed the arm she was covering herself with.

Cali nodded as she bared herself. "Oh, they're just delightful, girl." She winked at Laney. "See, you've nothing to be ashamed of. Oh, come here and give me a kiss."

Laney didn't want to kiss Ms. Cali. She didn't like women that way. What she wanted was to leap out of the guest room window and be gone from here already. Ms. Cali could have Caspar; in fact, she could fucking keep him.

But once again, Laney felt herself compelled to do the older woman's bidding. In a daze, she found herself stepping up close to Ms. Cali, felt her arms extending to fling themselves around the woman's neck; felt her lips parting to receive Ms. Cali's tongue; felt . . .

Laney suddenly felt intense pain in her chest. At once, her trance cleared up and she screamed in agony and looked down at herself.

Oh my God! Oh my God! She had a bleeding hole in her chest. Ms. Cali's right hand was stuck deep inside her left breast and was fiddling about inside her chest.

Laney stared at Ms. Cali in incomprehension. "Wha . . . what . . .!?"

But then Ms. Cali jerked her hand back out of Laney's chest. Laney felt something come loose from its moorings inside her body, then watched the blood spurt massively out of her. The next moment she was staring at her heart, ripped out from her body and dripping blood down over Ms. Cali's forearm, which was now a horrible hairy and black texture.

"Bye, little girl," Cali said, tossing Laney's heart away into a corner of the room. "I hate any sexual competition where my men are concerned."

But I wasn't competing with her. I don't even wanna be here, Laney thought miserably as she collapsed to the floor and died.

Cali now turned and smiled at Caspar.

CHAPTER 38

Caspar

For a split-second—due to the horror of Laney's death—Cali's mind-control over Caspar Jenkins dissolved.

"You goddamn murderess," he screamed at her as she turned toward him after unceremoniously flinging Laney's heart away. "What did Laney ever do to you, you heartless evil bitch!"

Terrified now beyond his worst-ever nightmares, Caspar Jenkins tried to flee. But then Cali reestablished her mental control over him again, and suddenly he once more desired this evil and blood-spattered woman standing in front of him more than he'd ever desired any other woman before in his lifetime. Once more she was perfection. It no longer mattered that she wasn't human (he'd seen how her hands had transformed when she'd killed Laney), all Caspar knew was that his cock was hard for Ms. Cali and he wanted to fuck her to death, wanted to fuck her until he died.

"Come to me," Cali told him. "Come and make love with me!"

Goofy grin back on his face, he went to her and took her in his arms.

She laid her head on his chest. Just like Laney had done. She was nice and compact; again just like Laney. Caspar looked down at Laney. She lay untidily, her neck bent, her eyes wide and staring; the agony of her murder was etched on her face. She looked horrible and totally unattractive.

He looked away from Laney and instantly forgot about her. Cali had just knelt and taken his penis in her mouth.

Oh shit, Caspar thought with delight as her sweet lips and tongue pleasured him. *Head like this is to die for.*

CHAPTER 39

Samantha & Jack

Samantha had finally fought free of the hands choking her.

She and Jack had in the meantime rolled off the bed and fallen on the floor. Still locked in their life-and-death struggle, they'd rolled sideways towards the red ring, then back again when it had erupted with ceiling-high flames on their approach. Now, they were almost underneath the bed. The light from the once-more dying circle of fire revealed that only dust and dead roaches lay beneath the bed.

She and Jack rolled out again. She was holding his wrists, keeping him at bay while he snarled and spit at her, his eyes piss-yellow, his mouth dribbling saliva, his nostrils flared with rage. In his wasted yet murderous condition, Jack looked grotesque and disgusting; completely not the man she loved.

Samantha considered her problem: as a private eye she was an expert in self-defense. She was proficient in both karate and judo. The thing was, she didn't want to hurt Jack. She knew her husband wasn't in control of himself. At the moment Cali was controlling him, and if Samantha gave into her own violent urges and feelings towards the demoness and attacked Jack with the same intensity he was currently demonstrating towards her, she might very easily break some of Jack's bones.

They got to their feet again. He bent her over the bed, but she spun out of his grip and then ducked around him so that his back was to the bed instead. She stepped away from him. "Jack, Jack, try to break her control over you!"

His response was merely to growl and charge at her again.

This time Samantha reacted on instinct. As Jack reached her, she grabbed hold of him, twisted and launched him over her head. Right towards the red circle. He was already in flight before she realized what she'd done.

"Shit, no!" she yelled as the ring of flame flared up again. But she'd thrown him so fast that he'd crossed out of the circle before the flames hit the ceiling.

The flames died down. Jack lay on the bedroom floor stunned. Samantha hurried across the ring. So intent was she on reaching Jack's side that she didn't notice that this time the ring had remained dead as her feet crossed it.

"Honey, are you okay?"

She expected him to answer her with an animal growl. But instead, he nodded. "Yeah, thanks for launching me out of there. I really needed that."

She gaped in surprise. "You're alright now?" Jack's eyes were clear again; the rage had left his face. Now he just looked tired. Tired and older than his years.

"Yeah, darling, you got me out of the succubus's ring. You'll never know how grateful I am for that. That red circle is part of the source of Cali's power."

Samantha nodded. She was still worried though. She was delighted that Jack was fine now, yet bothered because she knew their enemy could return any minute now.

She helped Jack to his feet. "Baby, do you have any idea how to stop that woman?"

He nodded and pointed weakly to the dresser. "Yeah, we need to burn her bed. Get out the lighter and lighter fluid you found!"

CHAPTER 40

Casper

Caspar would never have believed sex could be this scary.

They were doing it on the guestroom bed. Cali had locked Laney's corpse out of sight in the en-suite bathroom so the sight of her didn't distract Caspar.

They'd started out with him on top, but now Cali was riding him. At first the sex had been good, and then it had gotten mind-blowing. But now . . . she was still giving him intense pleasure, but he'd realized that she was also leeching him.

Now he understood how Dray had wound up the way he was.

Caspar felt himself drain away into her, a little at a time, his muscles dissolving by some unknown mechanism and invisibly seeping out of him.

His terror had no negative effect on his sexual potency. Inside her vagina, he was harder than ever. He didn't want her at all now, but her control of his mind ensured that he wanted her more than life itself. He gasped with pleasure, then shrank a little. Then he gasped some more and shrank a little bit more. He knew he already looked starved and shriveled.

"Yes!" Cali moaned, looking down at him and clawing his chest with her fingernails till the blood ran. "I like you deep inside me like this."

Caspar lifted a hand to stroke her erect nipples. The hand was withered; an old man's. Not as withered as Dray's, but getting there fast.

What the hell am I gonna do? Caspar thought as more of his essence flowed from him into the succubus. *I gotta stop this or die!*

But there seemed no way to stop it. Ms. Cali was moaning with delight. Caspar had to admit that she was great in bed. She had a certain way of moving her ass from side to side as she slid down on his cock, circling it around, that kept threatening to make him come.

Caspar didn't want to come. Not with Ms. Cali. Because, he already knew now, from endearments she'd whispered in his ears, that he would die the moment he ejaculated into her.

Caspar didn't want to die. Not like this. Not as young as he was. During the sex he flung confused glances over at the bathroom door. *Laney. Shit! My baby's dead! She's dead, and maybe Dray's dead too now, from when Ms. Cali flung him inside the living room. And I'm gonna be next.*

But something was odd though. Despite all of Ms. Cali's delighted moaning as she rode him, Caspar got the feeling that she wasn't entirely there with him. Occasionally her eyes lost focus and her sexual rhythm stuttered for a moment. Her attention seemed divided, like she was in conflict with herself.

But, oh shit—how sweet her pussy was!

Caspar suddenly felt his orgasm approaching. He tried with all his might to stop himself thrusting, but it seemed utterly impossible. His hips had a mind of their own. His hands gripped Ms. Cali's hips and he pumped her harder than before, his eyes widening in horror at his inevitable fate.

Shit, I'm gonna die! I'm gonna die!

But then, just when it seemed like nothing on Earth could stop him pouring away his life into this evil woman's body, Ms. Cali spat down on his chest, growled, "NO, NO, NO, NO and NO!" and vanished from on top of him.

Caspar was left staring down at his erection, while his heart beat like a drum. He was already the point of no return though. He watched his penis spurt semen three feet high in the air, then fell back in a dead faint.

"Shit—I'm still alive," he muttered, as consciousness left him.

CHAPTER 41

The Final Showdown

Samantha got out the lighter and can of lighter fluid from the drawer. She clicked the lighter on to ensure that it was working properly. She smiled at the small plume of blue flame the lighter produced.

"Is there any special way we need to do this?" she asked her husband.

Jack was seated on the floor beside the dresser, with his back against the wall. He shook his head at her. "Not that I know of. Just drench it with the lighter fluid and set it ablaze." Then he sighed. "Shame about the house though, I kinda like this place, what with the lake out front and everything. They even have a lake club with great fishing and lots of fun."

Samantha grimaced at him. "Forget it. After this debacle, you're moving back up to Cheat Lake with me. One lake's much like the other."

"Alright, darling, whatever you say." He pointed at the bed. "Better get started though. We're wasting time. That crazy supernatural bitch is connected to the damn bed. She'll certainly be back any second."

"Yeah." Samantha started towards the bed.

Cali instantly appeared in front of her, blocking her way. "The crazy supernatural bitch is already back," she said, frowning.

Now Cali looked serious as hell—her facial expression contained not the slightest trace of her previous games of sexual one-upmanship with Samantha. Her blue eyes were cold as ice, and while Samantha and Jack watched, her eyes altered their color to a bright glowing yellow, without either iris or pupil.

"I warned you not to mess with me," Cali said. Then she pointed at the objects Samantha was holding in her hands. "What do intend doing with those?" She laughed loudly. "I'm from Hell and you intend to *burn* me? How dumb of you."

"Not you, bitch," Jack called from behind Samantha, while staggering to his feet. "But your damn bed."

The faintest trace of worry flickered across Cali's face, but she quickly regained control of herself. "Ha ha ha!" she laughed. "The bed is nothing! I am the source of my own power!"

"You're lying," Jack said, stepping up beside Samantha and staring Cali coldly in the eyes.

"Even now I control you both," Cali insisted, her eyes glittering that horrible yellow. "Jack, on my command you will kill your wife."

"Hell no, I won't kill her. I frigging love her!"

"Do it! I order you to kill her."

Samantha looked really nervous now. She stared sideways at Jack, wondering if he'd really attack her again.

But Jack just laughed. "Forget it, Cali—that game's over. You forget that I was in the bed. I know all of your dirty little secrets." He turned quickly to Samantha and explained: "She can't control you once I'm outside of the ring. She needed me to remain in there in her place— but now that I've left the ring, her power's weakened."

Cali at first looked enraged, but then she nodded: "No, I can't control either of you anymore. But I can still kill you both . . . and I will now."

With that statement, both of Cali's forearms altered into black apelike forelimbs tipped with long claws.

Samantha gasped at the sight. Cali laughed. "Surprised, little wife? Yes, I'll kill you first—your husband will watch you die. And then I'll put him back on that bed and resume my takeover of this town."

"Like hell you will," Samantha growled back at her. "You've done more than enough harm already."

"Not as much as I plan on doing." Her yellow eyes beaming with malice, Cali launched herself at Samantha.

Samantha waited and went into a crouch, preparing to throw Cali like she'd thrown Jack. The succubus would clearly have no knowledge of judo or other self-defense techniques.

But then, just before Cali would have hit Samantha, Jack bowled into the succubus and knocked her over.

"Sam, hurry up and burn the bed!" Jack yelled over his shoulder as he and Cali went down in a fighting, snarling heap.

Samantha took one look at Cali and Jack rolling around on the floor, then terrified, she hurried across the red circle to the bed.

Behind her she heard Cali growling like an animal on the kill and Jack yelping like he'd been hurt, but she didn't look back. She didn't dare to look back. Instead, she focused on the job to be done. She squirted the lighter fluid all over the bed clothes and mattress and pillows and set the bed on fire. Then, once the purple/blue flames had begun spreading, Samantha quickly hurried around the bed, squirting more of the lighter fluid on each of the four bedposts. Then, for good measure, she flung both the can of lighter fluid and the lighter itself onto the burning bed and darted back outside the red circle.

She discovered she'd made her exit just in time. As she stepped outside of the circle, it spurted up in a wall of flame that obliterated the bed from view.

Samantha stared at the burning circle for a while, then she realized that behind her Cali had begun screaming.

She turned. Jack lay on the floor with blood coming from several slashes across his chest and belly.

Cali however, was on her feet and screaming. "NOOOOO!" she howled "NOOOOO!"

Skirting around Cali by a wide margin, Samantha hurried over to Jack's side and helped him sit up. She was relieved that he was still alive.

Together they watched as Cali began dissolving. This happened in quick stages, each following rapidly upon the heels of the next. First, her exterior appeared to crack and fragment, then the resulting powdery substance liquefied, and then the woman turned to gas. All through her transformation the succubus maintained her shape so that at the end she appeared as a transparent version of herself. And meanwhile, her yelling voice had been altering too, fading as her body did.

The expression on Cali's face was one of frustration and horror.

Meanwhile the fire in the bedroom was still raging. However, there was very little smoke, and Jack and Samantha didn't even think the flames were affecting the ceiling.

Then, Cali suddenly howled "NOOO!" again; after which her ethereal form broke apart into sheets of gas, and then, as if drawn into a vacuum cleaner, was sucked off into the raging ring of fire in the middle of the room.

"NOOOOOOO!" came Cali's voice once more, but its sound was weak now, fading to nothingness. As it faded away, so did the ceiling-high ring of fire. The fire reduced till finally all that was left were a few yellow flames dancing around the red circle, and then even those faded.

In the middle of the circle all that remained was a heaped pile of ash.

"It's over," Jack told Samantha, hugging her tightly to him.

"And I'm glad as hell it is," Samantha agreed, hugging him back tightly and shuddering. "She had me really scared. I thought she was gonna kill us both."

"You, a tough private eye? Scared?"

"Yeah, though I'll only admit it to you." Then she seemed to remember herself. She pulled away and stared at him in horror; at the mess of bleeding scratches that marred his torso. "Oh, I'm so sorry, darling, we need to get you to a doctor."

"I'll be fine," he groaned, rising to his feet with her assistance. He kissed her. "Honey, see if the door's open." She turned to go do so, but then he pulled her back and kissed her again. "And promise me one thing . . ."

"What's that?"

"That we won't ever stray this far from one another's side again?"

She pouted, then held him tight and kissed him and kissed him. "Yes, darling, yes, I do promise; and this time I really mean it. Though I guess this means we're gonna need to make some changes in our lifestyles."

He nodded. "For sure. Just don't keep leaving home. This Cali nonsense would never have happened if you were in the house with me."

She frowned at the thought that he was blaming her for everything that had recently happened to them. Then, seeing the smile on his face and realizing he was just teasing her, she laughed. "Whatever you say, captain!"

Jack growled in pain then. Samantha stared at his many dripping cuts, then propped him up against the wall. She left him leaning there and went to check the bedroom door. It opened easily. She returned and helped Jack across to it.

Before exiting the bedroom, they both looked back at the pile of ash in its middle. To their surprise, the previously glowing red ring around the ash-pile had now faded completely from sight.

They turned and left the north bedroom.

"Shit," Jack said, as they descended the stairs to the living room. "I wonder where the hell Cali's gone now."

"Anywhere is fine with me," Samantha said. "So long as she stays there and never comes our way again."

EPILOGUE

There was a huge mess to clear up. The police had lots of questions, but no answers. Once they felt well enough to speak, the four male survivors from the Crannson residence—Jack, Caspar, and the two other victims in the living room—gave their stories. (Dray Springer having regrettably died from massive internal bleeding after Cali threw him violently back into the living room.)

The police doubted everything they heard, but recorded it anyway, and then looked for a logical explanation instead.

In the end, the police labelled all the deaths (particularly those of Robin Thurgood and Laney Springer, who'd both had their hearts torn out) the work of a 'female nymphomaniac sociopathic thrill-killer.'

When Jack, now convalescing back up north at Cheat Lake, heard that description, he scowled, then remarked to Samantha:

"Yeah, that description just about sums up Cali."

The End

ABOUT THE AUTHOR

Gary Lee Vincent was born in Clarksburg, West Virginia and is an accomplished author, musician, actor, producer, director and entrepreneur. In 2010, his horror novel *Darkened Hills* was selected as 2010 Book of the Year winner by *Foreword Reviews Magazine* and became the pilot novel for *DARKENED - THE WEST VIRGINIA VAMPIRE SERIES*, that encompasses the novels *Darkened Hills, Darkened Hollows, Darkened Waters, Darkened Souls, Darkened Minds* and *Darkened Destinies*. He has also authored the bizarro thriller *Passageway,* a tribute to H.P. Lovecraft.

Gary co-authored the novel *Belly Timber* with John Russo, Solon Tsangaras, Dustin Kay and Ken Wallace, and co-authored the novel *Attack of the Melonheads* with Bob Gray and Solon Tsangaras.

As an actor, Gary has appeared in over seventy feature films and multiple television series, including House of Cards, Mindhunter, The Walking Dead, and Stranger Things.

As a director, Gary got his directorial debut with *A Promise to Astrid.* He has also directed the comedy feature film *Desk Clerk* and the police drams *Dispatched.*

GARY LEE VINCENT'S
DARKENED
THE WEST VIRGINIA VAMPIRE SERIES

DARKENED HILLS

When evil descends on a small West Virginia town, who will survive?

Jonathan did not start out his life to become a rambler, it justworked out that way. William was a troubled youth with something to hide. Both were from Melas, a small town tucked away in the West Virginia hills... a town where disappearances are happening more and more frequently.

After the suicide of a wanted serial killer, the townsfolk thought the nightmare was over. But when a centuries-old vampire is discovered they find out the hard way it's just getting started. Dark secrets can only stay hidden for so long and when the devil comes to collect, there will be hell to pay. Can Jonathan and William find a way to stop the vampire before it's too late? Find out in *Darkened Hills!*

DARKENED HOLLOWS

In the heart-stopping sequel to the award-winning *Darkened Hills*, Jonathan and William must return to West Virginia to face possible criminal charges stemming from their last visit to the damned town of Melas, where both had narrowly escaped the clutches of a vampire seethe.

And as livestock start mysteriously getting murdered with all of their blood drained, worried farmers are searching for answers - leaving the local Sheriff and his deputy racing against time to learn the cause before a more violent crime is committed.

Burning Bulb
PUBLISHING

WWW.DARKENEDHILLS.COM

GARY LEE VINCENT'S
DARKENED
THE WEST VIRGINIA VAMPIRE SERIES

DARKENED WATERS

When the world goes to hell, the chosen must arise!

As Talman Cane orchestrates a flood of epic proportions in this third installment of the *Darkened* series the towns of Melas and Tarklin are caught completely off guard by the deluge. Hell-bent on finishing what they started, the evil brothers return to the lunatic asylum to take care of the witnesses and add to the ever-growing army of the undead.

Aided by Lucifer himself and the insane vampire demon Legion, the stage is set to channel all of the forces of hell to come forth. In an all-out race to survive, Jonathan, William, and Amanda soon discover they are up against impossible odds as Lucifer opens the Gateway to Hell, ushering in the zombie apocalypse and the End Times.

Find out who will survive this cosmic battle of the ages in *Darkened Waters*!

DARKENED SOULS

Melas and the Madison House are about to be rebuilt.
True evil is about to be reborne!

Young ex-priest and vampire-killer William is drawn back to the West Virginian town that almost killed him, where his vampire arch-enemy Victor Rothenstein still stalks the earth.

The town of Melas lies destroyed after the battle of the End of Days. But why is wealthy Jackie Nixon so eager to rebuild it using the bone dust of murdered souls?

Terrible evil has visited before, but the Gateway to Hell is about to be reopened in a horrific climax. And this time – it's personal.

WWW.DARKENEDHILLS.COM

Burning Bulb

GARY LEE VINCENT'S
DARKENED
THE WEST VIRGINIA VAMPIRE SERIES

DARKENED MINDS

Jackie Nixon intends to become Vampire Queen, but at what blood-drenched cost?

In this continuation to the explosive infernal saga begun in Darkened Souls, newly-turned vampire Jackie Nixon is taking no prisoners. Accompanied by her daughter, Kate, and by the captive vampire lord Victor Rothenstein, Jackie Nixon explores the Darkness. There, she intends to rouse the slumbering vampire race, bound under an ancient curse, and with their help, rule the human world.

But there's a deadly threat to Jackie's plans. Not just William who is trying to stop her, but her own royal ambitions. If Jackie performs the ritual to wake the sleeping vampires the wrong way, she could instead free the Red Beast of Hell, an unspeakable evil that even the undead fear.

DARKENED DESTINIES

With over 45 people missing after Jackie Nixon's party, the mysteries surrounding Melas and the Madison House keep getting darker.

Now, with legions of vampires at her command, can anything or anyone stop her from gaining complete control over all mankind?

The final battle has begun! As the Vampire Queen ascends her throne and sets to unleash the full forces of darkness, the fate of all things good hangs in the balance.

WWW.DARKENEDHILLS.COM

www.ingramcontent.com/pod-product-compliance
Lightning Source LLC
Chambersburg PA
CBHW070935250626
47159CB00009B/3255